THESE WONDROUS MOMENTS

A Fates Short Story Collection

WHITNEY L. SPRADLING

Midnight Tide
PUBLISHING

TO MY FAMILY...

You should be used to seeing this by now. If you continue to ignore it, shame on you.

Once again, I beg you, if you are in any way related to me, please put the book down. I really hate awkward encounters, and that is exactly what will happen the next time we see each other if you read this book.

I appreciate the support, but DO NOT READ THIS BOOK!

Thank you.

CONTENT WARNING

This book contains adult themes that may not be appropriate for all audiences. These themes include: graphic sexual scenes, language, drug/alcohol use, mention of torture, blood play, and mention of past non-consent encounters and sexual assault.

These Wondrous Moments takes places after the events of the Fates trilogy and should be read after. If you haven't read the trilogy yet, please begin with the first book, These Dangerous Fates.

National Domestic Violence Hotline

If you or someone you know needs help, please call the National Domestic Violence Hotline at 800-799-7233.

You are not alone. Help is available.

For those who have overcome even the darkest of times. It's time to enjoy your happily ever after.

Our Dearest Ellis,

   Kitten, life hasn't been easy for you. You've gone through more than any person should ever have to. Our one wish is that we could have been there to stop it before it started. But watching your transformation, seeing you gain your wings and freedom, has been our greatest joy. Being able to stand next to you through the hardest moments of your life has been our honor.

   Love, we can't wait to live this life with you. Through every season we can rewrite the story and give you the memories you deserve. Every season that passes whether good or bad, we'll survive because we have each other.

   Baby girl, we know you'll continue to make us proud, and we'll continue to love and cherish every moment we get to spend with you. So celebrate the life you've earned, and we'll be next to you the entire step of the way.

Forever Yours,
Your Vampire Prince, Your Protective Alpha,
and Your Sweet and Caring Mage

WINTER

Ellis

"I have no fucking clue what to get her," I grumble to Allie as we walk down the street, bundled in our coats. "What do you get someone who has been held captive by a sociopath for half of their life?"

Allie sighs, her breath fogging in front of her. "Shit, I have no clue. Maybe books? Something she can lose herself in?"

"Maybe. I mean, I lost all interest in reading when I was going through my ordeal. But, I guess it's better than nothing?"

"We can at least check out the bookstore. At the very least we can buy ourselves something!"

I laugh and link my arm with hers. "Always the optimist."

"How is she doing?" Allie asks, sobering.

I shrug. "About as well as can be expected. I don't think she'll ever fully recover from it. She's doing better about being around more people, but men still make her nervous." I shake my head, my heart squeezing for everything my sister has gone through. While Sam didn't treat her the same way he treated me, she was surrounded by guards who leered and made comments. Not to mention all the torture at Sam's hands. "I don't know. I just wish there was something I could do, but I know it's just going to take time and patience."

Allie squeezes my arm where hers is linked with mine. "You're doing everything you can, El. Don't beat yourself up over it. She might not say it, but I know she appreciates everything."

I swallow back the lump that tries to choke me. It's been three months since I killed Sam. Three months since I freed my sister from his cruelty. Three months since I freed *myself* from that monster's clutches. A weight has been lifted. I finally have relief and comfort I hadn't known since before my mother's death. Killing Sam didn't solve every problem. I still have moments of panic and wake from dreams screaming and sweating. But my guys are always there to bring me back down. To remind me I'm safe. Loved.

We're still fighting for humans and weaker magicals. It's a fight we'll probably always be fighting, but it feels good to be doing something. And doing it with my Shields by my side has been everything I've ever needed. Learning how to live again, how to be normal—or at least as normal as I can be when I'm a Harpy with three mates—has been fun. Stressful at times, but truly an amazing experience.

Allie and I push into the bookstore. Warmth surrounds us, thawing our frozen exposed skin. Winter in Altair is brutal with the icy wind blowing off the river and streaming between the buildings. I stomp my feet, trying to regain feeling in my toes despite the fur lined boots Sterling bought for me.

Allie grins. "Meet back up in thirty?"

"Thirty minutes will do some serious damage to our bank accounts." But I grin back and we separate, each going to the section of books we prefer.

Allie is a mystery and thriller lover. I prefer romance. The spicier the better. But before I head to that section, I browse the aisles for something my sister may possibly like. We were so young when everything happened. I have no idea what her taste in books would even be, but I find myself in the inspirational section, and while it might be cheesy, it feels right.

My fingers brush the spines of books, not really reading the titles, but trusting my Harpy instincts. Something inside me tells me to stop, so I pull out the book my fingers rest on. A collection of inspirational quotes. Better than a book about healing and learning to live with your trauma. I tuck it under my arm and turn to head toward the romance section.

Before I get there, I pass a row of poetry books. Gracie used to love to write poetry. I walk down the aisle, stopping when I feel like I should, and tug a book off the shelf at random. The cover is beautiful with flowers and stars, so I add it to the quote book. And then I find the crown jewel. On the endcap of the poetry aisle is a selection of notebooks. A deep purple leather notebook with golden stitching and shiny golden edged paper catches my eye. I grab that as well. Maybe she'll be able to journal her way through her trauma. Or start writing poetry again.

With my sister's gift selected, I head to the romance section to do some serious shopping.

THE FIRST THING the guys did after things settled down was have a driveway put in so we didn't have to drive over the rocky terrain to get to the cabin. So, Cade's red Corvette smoothly climbs the mountain. Despite my first attempt at driving being an epic fail, Cade is a great teacher, and it only took me a few weeks to get the hang of it, and now he trusts me enough with his car to let me borrow it. It's nice to have this bit of freedom. Something I've never had before in my life.

The cabin comes into view, the sun just starting to sink below the horizon, and I grin. "What's this?" I ask, climbing out of the car with my bags.

Sterling waves his hand toward the house. "We're decorating for Christmas. Wanna help?"

"I don't know, guys," Cade says, eyeing my bags. "We might

need to return all of the decorations just to pay for the books she bought."

I flip him off as I walk past, swaying my hips enticingly. "I'd love to help. You could use some pointers, anyway."

I set the books just inside the door and when I return outside, Kai takes a chair from the porch and puts it in the yard, facing the house. "Your throne, my queen." He bows dramatically with a grin. "You can sit here and direct us peasants where to put the decorations."

I spend the next two hours, wrapped in a blanket with an endless supply of hot chocolate, and watch my guys string lights and hang garland. Sitting back and watching them bicker and tease makes my heart swell. And Kai wearing a Santa hat makes me chuckle every time I look at him.

By the time they're done I can't say they did a good job, but it's festive. The lights are droopy in places, the garland is wrapped asymmetrically around the porch pillars. A sad looking gingerbread man made of lights is about to lose an arm, and poor Frosty's hat won't stay on his head. It's a bit messy. Sloppy even. But I love it.

"I bought a tree and a bunch of ornaments, too," Sterling says tugging me inside. "Do you want to put it up now or later?"

"Now, please." I can't keep the smile off my face.

Kai steals me from Sterling and wraps me in his arms, pulling me to his chest. "It's our first Christmas together," he says, lips brushing against my temple. "I knew that would make you happy, but being able to actually sense the joy this brings you is truly special."

I don't have the words to tell him how this makes me feel. My first Christmas with my guys, totally free and able to live my life. Luckily, I don't have to find the words. Kai can sense it all. He kisses me gently, and I melt under his touch.

"Gross," Cade says, slipping a hand between us and shoving us apart. "Get a room."

I bite my lip and giggle, stepping away. With the three guys, the tree is assembled in record time and we get to work hanging the generic ornaments Sterling bought. When it's done, we all step back to admire our work.

"Not too bad," Kai says.

"It's just missing one thing." Sterling hands me something wrapped in white paper.

I peel the wrapping away to reveal a delicate spun glass golden feather. It catches the light as I hold it up, and my breath sticks in my throat. "It's ... beautiful," I whisper.

Sterling leans over and kisses my cheek. "Seemed appropriate for our first tree."

I squeal as Sterling crouches down and shoves his head between my legs. He stands, making me grab his hair for support as he lifts me onto his shoulders. Once I have my balance, I place the feather on the top of the tree where everyone will be able to see it. I'm pretty sure my smile will remain permanently on my face this entire holiday season.

CADE

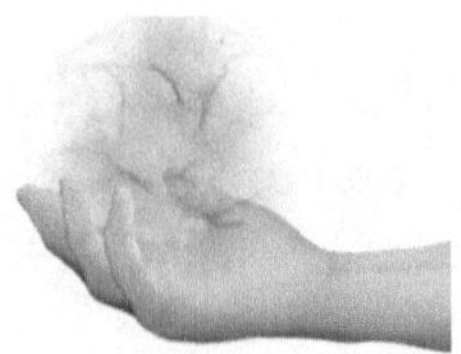

"HOW'S YOUR MOM?" KAI ASKS QUIETLY, NOT WANTING to disturb Ellis or Sterling.

After we decorated the tree, we sat on the couch and drank spiked hot chocolate and bathed in the Christmas lights while talking. None of us even paid attention to how long we lounged around and chatted until Ellis fell asleep, and Sterling not long after her.

Now, she leans against my shoulder with my arm around her middle and her legs thrown over Sterling's lap. Kai's on the floor between my legs with his head resting on my thigh. His hair is like silk as I glide my fingers through the strands.

"I think she's doing a lot better," I say, just as quietly. "Getting an apartment helped. It made her feel like she has more of a say in her life. Something she's not used to. And my sister being there has made it possible." I pause for a second, thinking through how to say what I want. "I told her about Ellis. All of it. The Harpy thing, the Shields, the mate bonds with all three of us." I bite my lip, hesitating. "I told her about you."

He lifts his head up to look at me, his gray eyes bottomless and breathtaking. "You did?"

"Yeah. She asked me a lot of questions and seemed to be pretty curious."

"Good curious? Or bad curious?" He searches my face for any hint at all.

"Good curious. She said one day she wants to meet all of you, especially you and Ellis, but she's just not comfortable with people yet."

He nods and lays his head back, but I don't miss the smile that turns up the corners of his lips. "And what about your sister? I mean I know she's giving Cole hell, but has she said anything to you about it?"

I snort softly. "Poor Cole. I don't envy him at all. Chloe has always been sassy and headstrong. I can't even imagine all the grief she's giving him. But we haven't talked a lot about it. I want to give her time to figure it out. I think she's coming around though."

"Are you two doing okay?" he asks. "I know it was a little strained at first."

"Yeah. It was weird being an adult around her. I was so young when she was taken, and I think I was worried about what she'd think about me. Like, what kind of a person I grew into."

Kai pinches my calf before looking at me. "How the hell could she not see you for the person you are? Caring. Selfless. Brave. There is nothing for her to not be proud of."

A lump grows in my throat, and I swallow it. Kai's eyes glimmer as he no doubt picks up the emotion swirling in me.

"I mean it," he whispers, sitting up straighter. "I couldn't be more proud to stand next to you. As Ellis's Shield, as your friend, as your ... more than friend? What the hell are we? Lovers sounds too fucking weird."

I chuckle. "Family," I say, tightening my grip in his hair, like if I hold on hard enough he won't disappear.

It's only been three months, and the fear still hits at random moments. The worry that one of them might not be there when I wake up in the morning. The uncertainty that the future will be stolen away from me. I know I'm not the only one who still struggles with it. We all do, but Ellis does especially. And I'm not sure she'll ever really get over it.

Kai frowns as all of this is sent into the ether for his empath abilities to pick up. He pushes to his knees and leans into my space, his breath fanning over my mouth as he says, "Family. That sounds ... perfect."

Then he closes the distance and presses his lips to mine. I know he means for the kiss to be sweet, but I need more than that right now. When the fear hits, sometimes I just need to feel them. To know they are still with me, and will always be with me.

I run my tongue along the seam of his lips and he opens for me, letting me sweep in and claim him. His hands on my thighs tighten before sliding up to the waistband of my pants. I stop him and break away with a deep breath.

"Wait," I whisper, looking at Ellis and Sterling.

As gently as I can, I slide out from under her, laying her down and placing a pillow under her head. She murmurs something unintelligible before rolling over. Sterling opens his eyes and blearily takes in the scene. Without a word, he flops to the side, wrapping his arms around Ellis and burying his face in her stomach. They are both breathing deeply in seconds.

Kai and I watch them for a moment before he threads his fingers through mine and leads me upstairs. Anticipation swirls in my gut, thickening my cock already and we haven't even done anything. In the bedroom, he closes the door and backs me to the bed, fingers just barely grazing my hips, teasing the skin there and making me shiver.

"I'm going to make you forget every one of those fears." His breath is warm against my neck where he whispers the words, his lips a soft brush that has me aching for more. "I'm going to make you forget all of the uncertainty. I'm going to make you forget your own godsdamn name."

His words burrow deep into my bones, vibrating and resonating. With my hands under his shirt, fingers tracing his cool skin, I can feel his heart thumping madly behind his ribs. I know mine is beating just as hard in anticipation of what's to come.

He holds himself back, fingers always just barely touching, lips just barely hovering. It drives me wild, waiting for his touch, waiting for him to claim me. And as much as I want to growl at him to hurry the fuck up, I swallow my words and savor the slow build and increasing tension.

Letting go with Kai has always been so incredibly freeing. Being able to submit, to let someone else take control, gives me a sense of euphoria I can't find anywhere else. Not even with Ellis. I don't have to worry with Kai. I don't have to make sure I'm not hurting him. I don't have to worry about ensuring he finds his own pleasure. I can just ... be. Not that I don't love being with Ellis. Of course I do. I love being her protector. I love giving her pleasure and getting my own from her. It's just different with Kai. It always has been.

Kai's fingers move away from my hips, sliding up my abs, over my chest. At the same time his tongue licks up the column of my throat, and my head falls back.

"Arms up," Kai breathes.

My arms raise of their own accord because I'm pretty sure all coherent thought has fled. My cock aches, pressing against my jeans almost painfully, and I just want Kai to take it in his hand or mouth.

Instead, he lifts my shirt over my head, tossing it behind him to the floor. His fingers lazily trail over my shoulders and chest, white his lip and tongue graze my neck.

"What are you thinking about right now?" Kai asks, his voice low and dark.

"Your mouth around my cock," I gasp as I slide my hands up to tangle in his hair.

He chuckles, the sound snaking through me, making my stomach clench with desire. "Patience, my valiant mage, patience." One of his fangs grazes the sensitive skin just below my ear and I moan, cock throbbing.

"Kai," I breathe. I tug his hair, urging, pleading with him.

When his fingers finally undo the button of my jeans and tug down the zipper, my legs are shaking with unrestrained need. Kai tugs down my pants, freeing my cock, and kneeling on the floor in front of me at the same time.

Just the sight of him on his knees, his gray eyes watching me with hunger and something deeper, almost makes me come. And when he wraps his hand around my cock, his touch so cool against my warmth, I grit my teeth and thrust into his hand.

He luckily doesn't make me wait too long before licking up the underside of my length and taking the head into his mouth.

"Fuck, Kai," I breathe, tugging the strands of his hair in my fists.

He hums, and his eyes sparkle with delight, fingers digging sharply into my thighs. I'm so keyed up by his teasing, I'm already on the edge. And when his fang brushes my shaft, I happily fall.

Only all of my training and exercise keeps me from collapsing as my orgasm crashes through me. I thrust my hips against Kai's face, and he takes it all, swallowing down every last drop.

When Kai pulls away and wipes his thumb along his lower lip, fangs on display, I groan. My chest heaves, and my heart pounds, but despite my orgasm, desire continues to roar through me. I know more is coming. I know those fangs will find their way to my neck, and that thought alone drives me wild.

Kai stands and pushes me backward. I fall onto the mattress, sinking into the plush surface. He takes his time stripping out of his clothes, and if it weren't for the depth of the emotions in the room, I'd make a joke about him making a good stripper.

"Roll over, Cade." Kai pumps his hand up and down the length of his hard cock, piercings catching the dim lighting as he does so.

I do as he says, breath hitching. The bed dips as he kneels on either side of my legs, and I start when he drags one finger down my spine. He grabs my hips roughly and lifts them, and I let him. Enjoying the freedom of him taking control, and really enjoying the rougher side of him that comes out when he does it.

I close my eyes, burying my face in the sheets. Something about not being able to see what's happening heightens my anticipation, swirling my desires even higher.

I don't know what he does, but I don't hear the pop of the cap to the lube, so when his lubed fingers slide inside me, I groan in surprise, and bite the sheet between my teeth.

With my eyes closed, my other senses are heightened, and I can hear Kai's deep, uneven breathing. He's trying his hardest to restrain himself. Even the bed is trembling under his shaking.

"Do it, Kai. Fuck me." I say, breathing just as unevenly as him.

He snaps. The tip of his cock presses against my entrance, and I brace myself for him to push in. My fingers grip the sheets with each inch, and I force myself to breathe.

"Holy fuck," I gasp, doing my best to not lift my hips, letting him remain in control.

Kai manages to hold himself still for a total of three seconds. Then he moves. It's pure pleasure. And the sounds Kai makes as he fucks me, the way my cock rubs against the sheets, it doesn't take long for me to harden again.

With each one of Kai's sharp breaths, each grunt and moan, each slap of his hips against my ass, fire builds higher and higher in my veins, heating my blood.

Kai's pace falters and he stops with a grunt. "Fuck, Cade." He wraps a hand around my throat and hauls me up, pressing his chest against my back. "Cade," he breathes in my ear, my name like a prayer on his lips.

I let each one of my emotions free. All of the desire, the disbelief that he's mine, the love. I let him read all of it. "Yes, Kai."

He doesn't give me any warning. His fangs pierce my skin, and if it weren't for his grip on my hips and throat, I would collapse onto the bed, unable to move as my second orgasm barrels through me.

Kai keeps thrusting, and I feel his muscles tighten, his body taut as a bow string. He pulls his fangs from my neck as he shudders and groans out his own orgasm.

We stay like we are for a moment. His arms around me, my head back against his shoulder, his heart thumping hard enough for me to feel it. Kai softly kisses the bite mark, making me shudder from the oversensitivity, before he pulls away.

I fall forward, rolling at the last minute to avoid the mess I made on the sheets. I watch Kai through lowered lids, his hair disheveled, a flush to his skin that is usually absent.

"You can change the sheets," I mutter. "I blame you."

Kai huffs and collapses atop me. Tangling his legs with mine, and resting his head on my chest. "Anything for you."

I drift off to sleep with Kai's body on top of mine, and his lips pressing a kiss right over my heart.

ELLIS

"Great work today, Maggie," I say, smiling as the human woman packs up her bag. "You're really making a lot of progress. I'm proud of you."

Maggie smiles shyly, tucking a lock of red hair behind her ear. "Thank you. It's all because of you and Allie. You're great teachers."

"Will we see you next week?" I ask, following her to the front door of the gym.

"Yeah. I'll be here."

"Great. See ya then. Have a great Christmas!"

I lock the door behind her and flip the sign to *closed*. It was the last class of the evening and I have something I need to do. I text Allie and let her know I'm closing up and I'll be over in a few minutes.

Quickly, I wipe down the mats and punching bags, and toss the used towels into the washer. I'll start it when I come back in a few days. I love this job. More than anything, I love being able to help human women gain not only confidence but strength. I love giving them weapons they can use to protect themselves. But the next few days off for Christmas will be nice.

I finish my closing duties and set the alarm before stepping outside and locking the door behind me. The icy wind bites into my cheeks and fingers and chills my ears, but I don't put on my hat and gloves. I'm only going next door.

Allie has been splitting her time between the clinic and the gym. Oftentimes, women are uncomfortable seeing Cade, and Allie's presence helps to ease them. Every time he has to call and ask for her to step over for a minute, it makes me furious. Not that he is calling her over, but that there is a need for him to call her. I desperately hope one day Allie won't be needed to help calm these women.

The little bell above the clinic door chimes as I step inside. "Holy shit. It's freezing out there," I exclaim, stomping my feet.

"It's supposed to snow tomorrow," she says with a wide smile. "It hasn't snowed on Christmas in years."

"I know! I'm so excited. Everything feels so ... magical."

She ushers me into a private room, and I hop up on the table. "You sure about this?" she asks, studying me closely.

"Positive."

"I figured as much, just wanted to make sure." She smiles then begins gathering supplies. "Okay. Arm out."

I roll up my sleeve and hold my arm out for her. She prods my forearm with a gloved finger before wiping the area down with an alcohol pad.

"This will probably sting a bit."

I close my eyes and take a deep breath, not watching what she does. A second later, a sharp burning pain slices into my arm. I grit my teeth, but honestly, it's not that bad. I've had worse. Pressure as she prods the area, then a sharp tug that makes me gasp.

"That hurt," I grumble, blinking back tears.

"Sorry. That was the worst part. I'm done. Just a few butterfly bandaids and you'll be good to go. Shit. There are no bandaids in here. Hold this there, will you? Keep pressure on it."

I look down and press the cloth into my arm. Allie strips off her gloves and heads out of the room, so I hop down and make to follow her. Except she stops suddenly in the doorway and I crash into her back.

"What are you doing here?" she asks. "You're supposed to be off today."

"I forgot somethi—" Cade spots me behind Allie and his violet eyes widen.

Allie quickly ducks away, making herself scarce. I bite my lip and shuffle back and forth as Cade trails his gaze over me. He spots the cloth I'm holding to my arm and steps closer.

"What happened? Why are you here?" He tries to take my arm, but I pull away. "Ellis. What happened?"

"Nothing. I'm fine." My heart flutters in my chest. *Please don't pry. Please don't pry. Please don't pry. Just move on.*

He narrows his gaze at me and snatches my arm faster than I can blink. "You're bleeding, Ellis. That's not fine." His fingers gently move mine away from the cloth, and he lifts it up, displaying the two-inch cut Allie made. He goes still, not even his chest rises with breath. When he lifts his gaze to mine, his eyes are wide. "Ellis?"

"I wanted it to be a surprise," I say quickly, then wince. "Maybe I shouldn't have. I assumed the talk we had meant we were all on the same page, but maybe I should have made sure. I can have ano—"

He cuts me off with a raised finger wreathed in violet light. Gentle warmth pulses against my arm as he runs it over the cut, his magic healing the wound. "If we're going to have children, it would make sense to remove the implant." His voice is quiet and low.

"Cade, is this okay?"

His answer is a kiss. It's gentle. Sweet. But when he pulls aways, his eyes are burning so incredibly bright. My stomach flutters at the same time my core clenches. I know he's giving me the choice. Walk away now, or do this thing.

But what he doesn't understand is that when it comes to him, when it comes to any of my guys, I will always, always, choose them.

I stand on my tiptoes and clasp my hands around the back of his neck. "Kiss me, Cade," I whisper.

Something feral glows in his eyes, and I know his magic is right on the surface. When he picks me up, wrapping my legs around his waist, I feel his magic caress me. It slides over my shoulders, down my back, squeezing my ass. It heats my blood almost as much as his stare does. I never know anymore if it's him controlling his magic or if it's taken over and doing what it wants. The thrill of that, of knowing I'm buried so deeply in his soul even his magic can't resist me, it's empowering.

Cade carries me to his little office and kicks the door closed behind him. His chest is heaving, his limbs trembling slightly. "Are you sure? This could ... you could ..."

I kiss him and roll my hips as much as I can in his grasp. "That's the point of removing the implant," I say, pulling away. "We're doing this. Now."

He shudders, his magic flaring in a bright violet light around him, and he gently sits me on his desk. Right on top of the folders and papers. Eager, and needy, I unbutton his pants before sliding my hands under his shirt and up his stomach.

He mimics my movements, slipping his hands under my sweater and slowly teasing it over my head. My bra follows, and he leans forward, pushing me backward so I'm laying on the desk. It's cold against my heated skin, making me arch my back and gasp.

Cade slides his hands under me to the small of my back and he bends forward, sucking one of my nipples into his mouth.

"Cade," I breathe, tangling my fingers in his hair. "Please." My hips lift, begging him to get this moving.

He chuckles, but takes his time. Swirling his tongue, grazing his teeth, pinching the other nipple between his fingers. My body writhes under him as my nerve endings light up and burn brighter than fire.

When he finally tugs my jeans and panties down, I can feel the slickness between my thighs. Cade stares and licks his lips, palming himself through his own pants.

"Fuck, I want to taste you, but I want to be buried deep inside you even more."

I watch him yank his shirt over his head, his muscles bunching deliciously. He smirks at me as he so very slowly tugs down his pants. Growing desperate, I spread my legs wider and slip my fingers through my wetness.

Cade's eyes darken as his pupils blow out, his hand fisting around his cock as he steps out of his pants. He watches me pleasure myself for a few seconds, my hips rising to meet each thrust of my finger.

I see the moment he's had enough watching. His cock twitches in his hand, another bead of precum leaking from the tip. He growls and slaps my hand away before lining up with my entrance.

My breath freezes in my chest as I hold it, waiting for the stretch and friction of his cock inside me. He doesn't make me wait long. I tip my head back as he slides inside, moaning and wrapping my legs around his waist, pulling him even closer.

Cade doesn't waste any time. His movements start slow and unhurried, but they don't stay that way. It doesn't take long for him to increase the pace to the point where the desk groans across the floor with each thrust.

Something inside of him has gone primal. His magic flows and eddies just under the surface of his skin, making him glow violet. His eyes shimmer and fracture with purple light. It's beautiful, and sexy, and I know exactly why it's happening.

Removing my implant has turned the magical creature he is into one intent on getting me pregnant.

I can do nothing but hang on and enjoy the ride as Cade's movements become even more fierce and dominating. And I certainly enjoy the ride.

Tendrils of his magic snake over my skin, wrapping around my thighs, brushing against my core. Cade stares intently into my eyes as his magic flicks over my clit multiple times. My orgasm rises and crests, waves of pleasure spreading through me.

Cade keeps moving, he keeps pumping his hips until my body stops its shaking. Only then does he unleash himself. His magic flares from him as his hips jerk in uncoordinated movements. He groans, his entire body shuddering as he comes inside me.

When he finally stills, we stare at each other. A moment passing between us that stretches endlessly forever, the depth of his love shining in his beautiful violet eyes.

"Ellis, love," he breathes, leaning down to kiss me.

I kiss him back. Still breathless. Still reeling. So incredibly in love with him.

"We should probably get going," he murmurs against my neck.

I hum, but don't move. My fingers graze his shoulders and arms, his skin is warm and his muscles are tight. I want to curl up with him, skin to skin, and lose myself in him again. But he pulls away slowly, as if he's forcing himself to move.

"We have the Christmas Eve party at Shari's." He stands above me, in between my legs, and stares down at me splayed on his desk.

His gaze travels over my body, and there was a time I would have tried to hide myself from that intense perusal of my body. But Cade—and the other two-—have done nothing but show me how beautiful I am. Now, my body flushes with heat, but not in embarrassment. It's the look he's giving me. The way his eyes are more dark blue than violent as his pupils expand. It's the way he swallows thickly and how his chest rises unevenly. It's the way he is affected just by looking at me.

"Cade," I whisper, just a little hint of begging in my voice. We can be late to the party. Shari won't mind.

He steps away, his movements jerky. "No. Don't tempt me, love. We can play later."

Only the wicked promise of his words gets me up and moving. I'm going to hold him to that promise.

Shari's house is warm and inviting as we pull up the drive. Garland wraps around the porch railing and the banister of the steps. A wreath hangs on the front door, the tails of the red ribbon blowing in the icy wind. Warm yellow light spills from the windows and pools on the ground outside, illuminating the snow that started falling not too long ago.

Kai parks the Hummer behind Chloe's white Prius, and we all climb out into the bitter wind. The guys follow me up the steps carrying presents and Cade's casserole, and Shari greets us at the door with a wide smile.

"Come in, come in," she says warmly, ushering us inside. When we're all piled in the entryway she wraps me in a hug. "I'm so glad you guys could come."

"We wouldn't have missed it for the world," I reply. Sex, sure, but nothing else would have stopped us from coming.

It smells amazing. Roasted turkey, spices, pumpkin pie. It makes my mouth water and my stomach rumble.

"It smells great in here, Mom," Sterling says, passing his pile of presents to Kai so he can give his mom a hug. "It reminds me of the times before Dad died." He kisses her cheek, and we all turn away to give them a moment.

"Ellis!" Chloe bounds up to me and hands me a glass of white wine. "Cheers." Our glasses clink and we both take a sip before she links her arm with mine and tugs me away. "What's new? I haven't talked to you in a few days."

"Well," I drawl, looking around to make sure the guys are out of earshot. "I had my implant removed today."

Chloe gasps. "Are you trying to get pregnant?"

"Not trying, necessarily. But when—if—it happens, it won't be unwanted." I smile at her, one hand on my stomach like I can already imagine a little magical creature growing in there. "I mean, we don't even know if it's possible. More than likely, if I do get pregnant, it will be a wolf."

She nods in understanding. Mages who mate with other species produce non-magical babies. Vampires rarely reproduce anyway, and always only with other vampires. Shifters—wolf shifters, at least—have a higher chance of reproducing with another species just because they are stubborn, and their babies are too.

"Well, with the amount of sex you have, I'm sure it will take no time at all." She winks at me, grinning wickedly.

My face heats, and I duck my head, letting my curls hide the blush.

She grabs my arm with her freehand. "You already had sex without it, didn't you? You had it removed today, and banged one —or more—out already."

I choke on the wine I just swallowed. And she just grins at me.

"Which one was it? Who's trying to be baby daddy number one?"

I give her a flat stare. "Do you really want to know?"

She blanches. "Ew. No. I don't need to think of my little brother that way."

"Not so little," I mumble, making her gag. "But, all that aside," I say, laughing, "What's the latest on the Cole situation?"

She sighs, taking a long drink of her wine. "I feel it, you know? The connection. It's very clearly there, and it tugs at me incessantly."

"Yeah, it does that. Sterling was so good at ignoring it, and it drove me wild."

She smiles coyly. "It's fun making him pursue me, letting him think I have no interest in him. And you're right. I can see how crazy he gets when I act like I can't feel the thing between us."

"So, you do like him?" I ask tentatively, not wanting to push her into talking about something she doesn't want.

She bites her lip for a moment, thinking. "I do. I think I do, at least. It's hard for me to accept that he's a wolf and not a mage, you know? I've always wanted a family, and if I accept the bond, I won't get that. But, I'm not sure I can reject it. I don't know which would be more painful. Not having children or not having ... him."

"Have you talked to him about all of this?"

She shakes her head. "We've had coffee a couple of times, but that's all I allow myself. It's hard to be around him and not be *with* him. The temptation to touch him, to kiss him, it's so strong. And I know if I let myself, I'll lose myself in him, and I won't be able to stop. So I've just been teasing him. Stringing him along and making him chase me."

"You should talk to him. When you're done making him work for it, of course. But you both need to talk about what it would mean, because he might have the same concerns."

Her eyes flare with fear, like the thought of him deciding he didn't want the bond is a wake up call for her.

"Start by dating. You don't have to rush into accepting the bond first thing. Get to know each other. Who knows, maybe you'll hate him."

She laughs, but I already know she's falling hard for Cole. And I don't blame her. If he's anything like his brother, which I suspect he is, he'll be an amazing mate. Looking over her shoulder, I see the guys watching us, Cole included, and I sigh.

"Come on. We should mingle before people think we don't like them. Plus, I need to give Gracie her gift."

ELLIS

THE SOUNDS OF MERRIMENT ARE DIMMED UPSTAIRS IN the hallway, although Sterling's booming laugh can be heard clearly. Cole's follows, and I smile. The brothers are so similar, and I'm glad they finally have each other.

Taking a deep breath, I knock on Gracie's door, her present clutched in my hand. Suddenly, I want to toss it down the stairs. Why did I get her an inspirational book and a journal? What a horrible idea.

"Gracie? It's me." I knock again and she slowly opens the door. "Hey." I smile, trying to not to scan her from head to toe to see how she's doing.

Her face is still gaunt, but it's not near as bad as it was three months ago. I still don't like how long it's taking her to gain weight. With Shari's cooking, she should be filling out a lot faster.

"Come in," she says, quietly, and moves out of the way.

The door closes behind me, cutting off the laughter from downstairs. I try to ignore the way my heart aches when I realize I'd rather be down there than up here. My family is down there. My mates, my friends, my ... in-laws-ish. That's a weird word to apply to Shari, Cole, and Chloe since I'm not married, but it's true. Gracie is my family, she's my blood, my sister, but she's so distant. It's almost like she's not even here.

I hate the thoughts and the guilt they make me feel. Gracie went through something horrible and she's healing. Just because it's not as fast as I want it to be, doesn't invalidate it. Just because Chloe and I are able to be around people and enjoy ourselves, doesn't make Gracie wrong.

I shake the thoughts from my head and sit on the edge of her bed. "Merry Christmas," I offer with a tentative smile.

The last Christmas we spent together, we were a family. A happy family. Mom, dad, presents, dinner, the whole thing. There was laughter just like there is downstairs. Conversation, warmth, love. In her room tonight, it's cold and lonely. It's not very Chistamas-y.

She says nothing, so I hold up her presents. "I got you something. It's not a lot, but hopefully you like it."

She doesn't take it, just stares at the wrapped gift in my outstretched hand. "I didn't get you anything," she says quietly.

"That's okay. I don't need anything." I shake the present for her to take, but she just eyes it with sadness. "Seriously, Gracie. I have everything I need. I'm just glad you're here." When she continues to stare, completely lost in her own mind, I set the present down and stand, my heart sinking as I do so. "I'll be downstairs if you want ... if you need anything."

I slip back into the hall, and Gracie lets me. I lean against the door and squeeze my eyes shut, pushing down the emotions that threaten to consume me. Now is not the time to deal with them, so I head back downstairs, into the light and laughter and love.

The rest of the evening passes in a blur of smiles, laughter, and delicious food. The snow continues to fall, and everytime I look out the window, I get the urge to go stand in it. So when I have a moment to myself, I do exactly that.

Shari stops me in the kitchen before I can step outside, though.

"Ellis? Are you okay?" she asks, concern threading her voice.

"Oh, yeah. I just wanted to go stand outside for a second. In the snow."

She smiles and nods, but comes to stand in front of me. "I just wanted to tell you how happy I am to have you in the family. You and the other boys. I see how happy you make Sterling, and there's nothing else a mother could ever want than her child's happiness." She takes my hands and squeezes. "I am so grateful to have you as my daughter. The hope you gave me before ..." she trails off and shakes her head. "Thank you, Ellis."

I blink away my tears and wrap my arms around her. She smells like vanilla and flour. "Thank you," I whisper. "Thank you for being a mother to me."

"I never want you to think I'm trying to replace your mom, but I'm glad I can be there for you." She steps away and turns to the counter. "Don't stay out there too long, I'm cutting the pie."

I laugh and step out into the frigid night air. It's so quiet outside. If I strain my ears, I swear I can hear each snowflake falling to the earth. The air is fresh and wintery. I can't describe the smell, but it smells like ... snow. My boots crunch the snow on the ground under my feet as I walk down the steps and into the yard. Wet flakes cling to my eyelashes and melt on my cheeks. I lift my face to the sky and close my eyes.

Arms wrap around me, warm and inviting. I didn't even hear Sterling approach. "You smell good," I say. "You always smell like winter." His scent mixed with the snow is almost intoxicating.

He chuckles, his breath fogging around us. "You smell good, too." He buries his nose in my neck and inhales, making my toes curl in my boots.

"It's fucking freezing out here," Kai complains, coming to stand on my side. "Why are you standing in the snow like idiots?"

"It's peaceful," I say. "Or at least, it was peaceful, until you opened your mouth."

"Kai ruining the peace. Sounds about right." Cade steps up to my other side, looking at Kai around me and Sterling.

"Watch it," Kai growls. "I bite."

"Oh, I know," Cade purrs.

I let their banter wash over me, closing my eyes and enjoying their warmth and their voices. When they quiet down, I say into the silence, "I had my implant removed today."

Sterling's arms tighten around me and Kai sucks in a breath. The silence deepens and I can practically feel all of their thoughts whirling through their minds. Kai reaches for my hand, threading our fingers together. Cade smiles at me, pure love and joy shining in his eyes. And Sterling holds me tightly.

I close my eyes and take a deep breath of the winter air. Perfect. An absolutely perfect moment.

THE HUMMER HAS no problem getting up the driveway even with the snow on the ground. The house looks beautiful in the freshly fallen snow with the Christmas lights and garland. I stand and stare at it all for a moment, committing it to memory. My first Christmas in my happily ever after era.

"Should we do presents now or wait until we wake up tomorrow?" Cade asks, climbing up the steps.

"Now," I say, darting past him, bouncing on my toes as Sterling unlocks the front door.

They all laugh, and we head inside. The only lights inside the house come from the tree. They reflect off the shiny wrapping paper and the wooden floor. I can't keep the smile off my face. Everything has been so perfect today. I couldn't have asked for a better Christmas.

Cade flips the lights on and I frown, but settle on the floor in front of the tree. I hand each of the guys their present from me, and sit back a little nervously as they each open it. I don't have a lot of money, so I struggled to find the perfect gifts.

Kai is first, and when he reads the card—the only thing he has to open—he laughs. "Cooking classes?"

"I thought they would be a fun date activity for me and you." I study his expression, searching for any disappointment. "Is it … okay?"

He smiles broadly, showing off his fangs, and he crawls over to me. "It's perfect, baby girl." He kisses me, then sits back.

Cade is next. He unwraps the box and opens it. His smile is blinding as he looks up at me. "You got me the hardback box set of a medical encyclopedia?"

"I thought you could put it on your bookshelf at work."

"I love it, Ellis. Thank you." He leans over and kisses me, brushing a finger down my cheek.

Sterling is next. "I get two presents?" His grin is evil as he rubs it in, looking at Cade and Kai.

"Just open them," I say with a smile.

He unwraps the biggest one first and holds it up.

"It's a bag for you to carry your clothes in when you shift. Fluffy will be able to carry it. That way no get's to see you naked. Only me." I grin at him, slightly possessive.

"Of course. We wouldn't want just anyone seeing me naked. Thank you, kitten. This will be handy for sure." He opens the smaller box and frowns as he holds up a stuffed squirrel.

"Fluffy deserves a gift, too," I say defensively. "It squeaks."

Sterling squeezes it and makes it squeak. "He'll love it. We can show him tomorrow. But first …" he trails off and pushes to his feet before pulling me up with him.

"Give me one minute," Cade says, jumping up and rushing out the front door.

I glance between Kai and Sterling, both of them grinning, but neither say a word until a horn sounds outside. They push me toward the door and out in the snow once again. Sitting in the driveway is a white Jeep. Cade jumps out and comes to me, dangling a keychain.

"Merry Christmas, love." His smile is so bright.

So are Kai's and Sterling's as I glance at them.

"You guys got me a car? A Jeep?"

"We don't mind you driving our cars, but we figured you'd like to have one of your own," Sterling says.

"And we remembered you mentioning you love Jeeps," Kai adds.

Cade places the keys in my palm. "It's all yours, Ellis."

The tears slide down my cheeks, warm against my chilled skin. I have no words to say to them. While they could have gotten me jewelry, or any number of expensive items, they chose something that signifies my freedom. They've given me the final piece to live *my* life, and it's more than I could have ever hoped for.

Spring

ELLIS

I PULL UP THE DRIVEWAY IN MY JEEP AND PARK IT IN MY usual spot. The tulips Cade planted last fall are starting to pop their green little heads above the dirt and they line the path to the stairs in spiky sentry. The air is still chilly, but the warmth from the sun promises warmer weather to come.

The renovations on the house are finally complete. I've been shopping and decorating my little library like a fiend. It's been a form of healing for me, to reclaim the thing I love most. I grab the bags from the back of my car, the most recent decorations I bought, and trudge up the steps.

I'm surprised to find Kai on the couch scrolling through his phone. It's still a little early for him to be up. I drop the bags on the floor, shaking out my hands and walk over to him.

"Good morning," I say, leaning down to kiss him.

He hums and tugs me onto his lap, deepening the kiss. "It certainly is a good morning," he murmurs when he finally pulls away.

I laugh softly, running my fingers through his black hair. When I take a breath, I catch a whiff of something smoky and acrid. "Is something burning?"

Kai's gray eyes go impossibly wide, and he throws me off his lap onto the couch. "My cookies!" he shouts, jumping up and dashing into the kitchen.

I scramble to my feet and follow him. Smoke fills the air, and I cough. I'm shocked the smoke detector hasn't gone off yet. I quickly open the window and flap a towel around to clear the air. Kai swears as he opens the oven and pulls out a tray, letting it clatter on top of the stove.

I step up next to him and stare. "What ... what was it supposed to be?" I know he said cookies, but that doesn't look like cookies. More like blackened crisps of cookie shrapnel.

"Chocolate chip cookies," he mutters.

I glance at him and find him sticking his lower lip out in a pout. "Okay, well something went wrong. Walk me through what you did."

He crosses his arms and glares at the supposed cookies. "I followed the recipe exactly. They looked perfect when I put them in. I'm positive the oven was set to the right temperature. I triple checked it. I set an alarm for halfway through and came in and flipped them, then put them back in to finish."

I gape at him, not sure I heard him correctly. "You ... you flipped them?"

He nods, frowning at me. "Yeah. So the other side could cook too."

My lips tug toward a smile, but I hold it back. I'm not sure I do a good job at keeping my voice from hiding the laughter. It shakes a little as I say, "You aren't supposed to flip cookies."

"But you flip pancakes."

"Cookies aren't pancakes, babe. They cook through because they are in the oven, where it's hot. Pancakes only get hot on the bottom so you have to flip them."

He narrows his gaze at me. "You're laughing at me."

"No I'm not, I'm ..." I trail off as he slumps away, and I grab his wrist, turning him to face me. "Kai. I'm sorry. I'm not laughing at you. I know how hard you're trying, and I admire that you're not giving up."

"I just ..." He pulls out of my grasp and leans against the pantry, sliding down to sit on the floor. "I just want to be of use to you."

My heart cracks at the despair in his voice. Sitting in his lap, I take his face in my hands, forcing him to look at me. "What does that mean, Kai?"

"Cade and Sterling provide for you. They cook for you and do things that you need them to. I'm just ... here. Useless. I can't even go out in the sunlight, so you have to work your schedule around me. I just feel like ... like a burden."

"Where in the world is this coming from, Kai? You are so not a burden. And let's be honest, Sterling doesn't cook. He makes sandwiches. There's a big difference. And the nighttime living, I don't mind it. I actually prefer it. I feel like I'm closer to you guys because of it. I don't have to share you with the rest of the world as much as I would if we lived during the daylight. I don't like sharing you guys."

He smiles, but it looks forced. "I just don't know what I'm doing for you. I feel like I don't have a purpose."

"You have no idea how much you do for me, Kai. You're the first person to make me laugh. Do you know how long I went without laughing? Even before Sam, I hadn't laughed since my mom died. You're the one who's able to pull me out of whatever funk I'm in and make me laugh." I brush my thumb along his cheek, staring into his gray eyes. "But, Kai, you are one third of my soul. If I didn't have you, I wouldn't be complete. I'd be wandering the world lost and missing something vitally important to me."

He searches my face like he's looking for the truth, and I let him see it all. I have to remind myself that even though he's immortal, even though he's this big, bad, scary vampire, he still has feelings and insecurities. And Kai has always been more vulnerable than others. Maybe that's the empath in him, but whatever it is, I need to remember to make sure he understands at all times that he is my entire world. All three of them are.

"I love that you're learning how to cook. I think it's fun, and it's something different for you. But I don't want you to do it just because you think it's a way of providing for me. Because you don't need to do anything to provide for me. You do that just by being you. My Kai. My beloved."

His face softens and he rests his forehead against mine. "Thank you," he whispers.

"I love you, Malakai Thorne. Even if you can't cook."

I move to straddle his waist, kissing him to make him forget this ridiculous notion that he's useless. It doesn't take long for him to succumb to his desire. His fingers tangle in my hair and he groans as I rock my hips against his.

"I'm sure this is a health code violation," Cade says, coming into the kitchen.

Kai laughs, and relief spreads through me seeing the glimmer back in his eyes. "Care to join us?" he asks, grinning wickedly at Cade.

Cade looks tempted but he shakes his head. "Can't. And neither can you." He raises an eyebrow at Kai, trying to convey a message.

"Shit," Kai says. "I forgot." He kisses me once, then stands, setting me on my feet. "Raincheck?" he asks.

"What are you two doing?" I glance between them and laugh at their attempt at looking innocent. "Whatever it is, please be careful?"

"Always," Cade says with a smile, leaning forward to kiss me.

They disappear outside, and I hear Cade's Corvette rumble to life. Sighing, I look at the mess Kai left in the kitchen and set to cleaning it up. I don't know what he does when he's cooking, but he certainly makes a mess. I'm just finishing when my cell rings. I see Sterling's smiling face and swipe to answer.

"Hey," I say with a smile.

"How's it going, kitten?"

"Pretty good. I just finished cleaning the kitchen. Kai tried to make cookies."

Sterling chuckles. "And he made you clean up the mess? I should kick his ass for that."

"I don't mind. Besides, he and Cade left. They were being weirdly secretive."

"They did? What time is it?" Rustling comes through the speaker, and before I can answer him, he says, "Oh shit. Hey, I have to go. I'll be home a bit later. Do you need me to pick anything up on the way home?"

I narrow my eyes and hum. "What are you guys doing?"

"Nothing. I just ... I have another meeting I forgot about."

"Uh huh, sure. You go do your thing. I'll be here. Lonely. All by myself. Missing my guys."

Sterling laughs. "That's tempting, but you'll have to try harder."

"Whatever," I huff. "I'll see you later."

"Love you, Ellis." He hangs up before I can say it back.

Whatever they are doing, I'm sure it has to do with me. They're always doing things to surprise me. Like for Valentine's Day, when they took me back to the lake for a candlelit dinner and a repeat of the first time. Or the random flowers they bring home. Or when they set-up a drive-in movie against the side of the cabin and Cade heated a small bubble of air for us to watch a movie with the snow falling all around us.

Instead of wondering and trying to think of all the possibilities, I pick up my bags and head to my library. The pale gray walls with gold and pink accents instantly loosens my shoulders. Peace settles over me, and I set my bags down and begin pulling things out to decorate.

Fake plants—because I can't keep real ones alive—little wolf statues, bats, and hearts. All things that remind me of my guys. I set a golden wolf statue howling at the moon on the coffee table next to a fake succulent and sit on the overstuffed pink couch.

If the guys are going to stay out and do secretive things, I'll hole up in my library and read. Sounds like a perfect way to spend my time.

"YOU READY?" Kai asks, popping his head into the bathroom.

"Almost," I smile at him in the mirror and put the finishing touches on my makeup. "There. Ready."

His gray eyes trail over my body as I turn around to face him. "You look amazing." He pulls me toward him and nuzzles his face into my neck. "You smell amazing, too."

I giggle and push him away. "Not now, Kai. We're going to be late."

"So?" He presses me backward against the wall, all of his body lined up with mine.

I try to remember why we have to leave, but it's hard with Kai invading my senses. "Kai," I protest, but it's breathy and weak. And his fingers trailing under my shirt, tracing the soft skin of my stomach only make it even harder to gather my wits about me. But somehow I do. "Kai," I say again, this time stronger. "Kai, we have to go."

He sighs, his breath warming the side of my neck, but he steps back. "I know. Next time we go out, don't look so fucking good," he mutters as he walks away.

In the Hummer, Kai keeps glancing at me from the corner of his eyes, and I can't help but smile. I'm not dressed particularly sexy tonight. Just a pair of ripped jeans, a white tee that shows just a sliver of my belly, a black leather jacket, and a pair of leopard print flats. I pulled the top half of my hair into a messy bun to keep it out of my face, and my makeup is simple.

"You should probably keep your eyes on the road," I tease.

His lips twitch, but his gaze once again travels to me. "I'm trying."

"Maybe I should drive then."

"You can drive on the way home. I'm having a hell of a time keeping my hands to myself."

I shake my head and put on an air of seriousness. "What were you guys doing the other night?"

"When?" he asks, face a mask of innocence.

"You know exactly what I'm talking about. You, Cade, and Sterling were out late doing something secretive."

"I have no idea what Sterling was doing, but Cade and I went on a date." His lips just barely twitch, and he blinks rapidly three times.

"Uh huh. You're a horrible liar, Kai."

"I am not!"

"Then what did you guys do?" I turn in my seat to more fully face him, crossing my arms over my chest like I'm angry.

"We uh ... we went to dinner and a movie."

"Dinner, huh? What did you eat?"

His hands grip the steering wheel a little tighter, and I have to fight to keep a straight face. "Steak."

"Oh. How was it?"

"A little dry, actually."

"*You* ate a steak? Seems a little suspicious to me."

"N-no. I didn't. That's just what Cade said." He swallows, his throat bobbing with the movement.

"Riiight. And what movie did you see?"

"That new one."

"Of course. That narrows it down."

"The one with that guy in it. And the cars. And lots of explosions."

"Seems memorable. Must not have been any good."

He shrugs. "It was okay." He pulls the Hummer into a parking lot and heaves a sigh of relief. "We're here."

I chuckle. "Whatever, Kai. Keep your secrets. I'm sure I'll find out soon enough."

He hops out of the Hummer and hurries to my side to open the door and help me down. "I have no idea what you're talking about," he says for a final time with a kiss. "What's the class tonight?" he asks, taking my hand and heading toward the building.

"Cake baking. I thought it would be a nice mix after all of the cooking classes. As funny as it is to watch you gag over raw chicken, I figured this could end up being just as funny."

Kai grunts. "Glad I can amuse you."

I wrap myself around his arm and laugh as he leads me inside.

Ellis

I'm floating in a cloud of bliss, surrounded by softness and warmth. I sink lower in the bed, tucking the blanket under my chin. Then someone is there, hand on my shoulder shaking gently.

"Wake up, Ellis."

"Mnrgh," I grumble, rolling over to get away from the obnoxious stimuli.

A low chuckle rumbles from whoever won't leave me alone. Their voice is familiar, but I don't want to climb out of the trenches of sleep to figure out who it is. Another shake on my shoulder, and I shrug it off.

"Ellis," the person breathes, much closer than I expected. Their breath fans across my neck.

"What?" I demand, jolting backward to get them away from me.

"Fuck!" the voice shouts.

"Did she just break your nose?" another voice asks.

Break his nose? The words bury deep inside of me and eventually register. I sit up with a gasp, looking around. Cade is standing next to the bed, smiling. Kai is setting a tray of breakfast food on the foot of the bed. And Sterling is crouching forward, hand on his nose with blood dribbling between his fingers.

"Sterling!" I reach for him, hands fluttering around him unsure what to do. "What happened?"

He stares at me with icy blue eyes. "You broke my nose. Again." His voice is nasally and muffled behind his hands.

My eyes widen, and I gasp. "I did? What did I do?"

"You headbutted me."

Cade tugs Sterling's hand away and violet light twines around his fingers. "Let me see." His magic spreads to Sterling, making him grunt, then it disappears. "There. All better, big guy."

Kai climbs onto the bed and sits next to me. "We can't even plan you a birthday breakfast in bed without you beating us up."

"What?" I glance between the three of them, Sterling wiping blood from his face.

"Happy birthday, baby girl." Kai leans over and kisses my cheek.

Birthday. I completely forgot about that. It's never been anything I celebrated. I never had any reason to celebrate another year of my life. Especially when I was wishing it would just end.

"We made you breakfast in bed," Sterling says, sitting on the other side of me. "Well, Cade and I did. Kai sulked in the kitchen complaining that we wouldn't let him help."

"We let him pour the coffee," Cade amends, sitting in front of Kai and patting his thigh.

My eyes burn and I blink back the tears building on my lashes. "You guys," I whisper, hand on my throat.

Cade settles the tray over my lap. Pancakes, bacon, scrambled eggs with cheese, and of course, coffee. There is enough for three, and Cade and Sterling pick up forks to join me. It's delicious. It's perfect. It's the nicest thing anyone has done for me on my birthday since my mom was alive.

When my belly is full and the plates are empty, Cade moves the tray and goes into the hall. He comes back with three presents. "Happy birthday, love."

I stare at the presents in front of me and bite my lip to keep from crying. The first one I open is wrapped perfectly in gold paper, the edges folded and taped neatly. It has Cade's name written all over it. Inside is a little black velvet box. My fingers tremble as I open it. Nestled in a bed of white silk is a thin rose gold band inset with four purple amethysts.

"Cade," I breathe. "It's beautiful." I pull the ring out, but before I can put it on, he takes it from me.

Taking my left hand, he slips the ring onto my ring finger. His smile is bright and his eyes—eyes that match the ring—shine with so much emotion. He says nothing, though, as he hands me the next present—a small pink bag.

My hands shake as I pull out another black velvet box. This one holds a thin rose gold band inset with four aquamarines. My eyes blur with tears as Sterling takes the box from me and slips the ring on my finger, nestling it up with Cade's. Then Sterling hands me the last present.

This one is very obviously Kai's. The purple paper is ripped and taped together like a three-year-old wrapped it. When I open the box, my tears stream down my face. Kai places the rose gold band with four gray spinel stones on my finger with the other two rings. I swallow the tears and blink my eyes because they are blurring my vision and I can't see the rings on my finger.

"We might not be able to officially get married, stupid laws, but that doesn't mean we can't unofficially be married." Kai kisses the top of my hand.

"Besides, our bonds with you are more permanent than any wedding vow," Cade adds.

Sterling takes my other hand. "But, we never got you a present when we accepted our bonds. These rings can be a symbol of our vows to you."

I stare at the rings, each one the same color as my guys' eyes. "Thank you," I breathe, clutching my fist to my chest like I can press these rings and their meaning deep into my heart.

"We love you, Ellis," Sterling says. "And we couldn't be more proud to be building this life with you."

A sob crawls up my throat, and I can't keep it in. They surround me, each one pressing a kiss to my lips, or cheek, or temple. And I spend the rest of my birthday morning cuddling with my Shields.

"Girl! Look at you!" Allie squeals as I hop out of the Hummer and dash straight into her arms.

"Believe it or not, Sterling bought it for me. I'm not sure how he does it, but he's better at buying my clothes than I am." I laugh as I pull away and tug down the skirt of my black dress. The strapless top is black lace, with just a black strapless bra underneath to cover the girls. The skirt is skin-tight satin, with an open zipper up the thigh, and in the space of the open zipper is more black lace. My ensemble is topped off with a pair of strappy black heels.

"You're kidding me," Allie says with a smile. "Connor bought me a pair of shoes for Christmas and they were so awful."

"You should have worn them tonight. I'm sure they would have looked great with that dress."

She snorts but runs her hands down the sparkly red fabric of her dress. "It's kind of exciting being able to go out and wear something that draws so much attention."

"It is. Gods, we never would have gone out like this before."

We link arms and walk down the street, a wall of muscle at our backs. Connor, Kai, Cade, and Sterling ensure no harm comes to us. For my birthday, all I wanted to do was go out to a club. As a human, I've never been to one. It was always too dangerous, not to mention Thomas Kennedy would have had a fit. So with the protection my men give me, I decided to go out and have fun.

Cade groans behind me, and I turn to look at him. When I realize his gaze is pinned ahead of me, I whirl around. Chloe is standing in front of the club wearing a two piece outfit that shows an incredible amount of skin. I crack a grin when I realize that's why Cade was groaning.

I dart ahead and give her a hug. "I think Cade wants to murder you because of what you're wearing. Or lack thereof," I say with a laugh.

"He can get in line." A rumbly growl from behind Chloe draws my attention. Cole is standing there with his arms crossed and his piercing stare glaring at Chloe.

She sighs and rolls her eyes toward the sky. "When he found out about this shindig, he insisted on coming."

"Someone has to keep her out of trouble," Cole says, making Chloe stiffen.

I laugh and link my arm with hers and my other arm with Allie's. "Let's not worry about the guys tonight. This is for us."

The bouncer in front of the club looks like he's going to say something, but one look at Kai looming behind us and he quickly lets us in. Instantly, the heat from the press of bodies inside surrounds me. The bass from the music thumps deep into my bones. The scent of sweat, alcohol, and drugs float through the air, making me grimace.

Kai leads us across the dance floor, his presence parting the crowd of people like he has the plague. He takes us straight to the bar and has a conversation with the bartender I can't hear over the pounding music, but it leaves the bartender pale and wide eyed. A threat, most likely, to make sure nothing gets slipped into our drinks. Kai passes his credit card over and leans in to talk next to my ear.

"Order what you want," he says loudly, a hand on my hip. "Sterling and Cole got a table in the back corner. We'll watch you from there." With a quick kiss on my cheek, he leaves.

I'm unable to suppress a smile. For the first time in my life, I'm alone in a club. Well, not truly alone, but the illusion provided by the guys stepping away is powerful. Allie orders three drinks, and hands one to me and Chloe.

"Let's dance!" she says, grinning as widely as I am.

We find a spot on the crowded floor and lose ourselves in the music and motions. I have no idea how much time has passed—only the fact I've had three strong drinks—when a male body presses against my back. I freeze for a moment, before the scent hits me a moment later. Cherries and spice.

"You're too fucking tempting out here," Kai growls in my ear, sliding his hands around my waist and pulling me hard against him.

I bite my lip and roll my hips, grinding against him to the beat of the music. A second later, Cade steps in front of me, pinning me between them. Dancing with them like this is hot as hell. I search for Sterling, and find him sitting at a table, watching us with hooded eyes. I wish he'd join us, but I know this isn't his scene.

They dance with me for two more songs before both giving me a kiss and heading back to the table with Sterling, Cole, and Connor. Allie brings another round of drinks and the three of us dance until sweat slicks our bodies. I haven't had this much fun in ... well, ever. Spending time with my girlfriends. Acting like normal girls. This is the best present the guys could have given me.

Connor breaks first. Having enough of watching us on the dance floor, he steals Allie away to a dark corner. I laugh and Chloe returns to the bar for more drinks. I dance by myself for a bit, hips swaying, putting on a secret show for my guys. I'm so focused on what I'm doing, I don't notice the guy that stops in front of me.

"You look like you're having the time of your life," he says loudly enough for me to hear him over the thumping music.

My throat closes up, but I nod my head and make to walk around him. He stops me by placing his hands on my hips and drawing me against him.

"I'm kind of jealous. I want to have as much fun as you are." He drops his head to my neck and I gasp when I feel his tongue slide over my skin.

I wedge my hands between us, my heart thundering in my chest, and attempt to push him away. "Stop," I breathe shakily.

"Oh, come on. Let's have some fun."

Before he can do anything else, he's yanked away from me. Kai steps between us and stares the guy down. "She told you to stop."

The guy shrugs and gives Kai a smile. "Just having some fun." He leans around Kai and looks me up and down.

Kai shoves the guy hard enough to make him land on his ass. "If you were smart, you'd keep your hands and eyes off my beloved."

I place my hand on Kai's back, feeling his trembling restraint, and he turns around. His eyes are ruby red, but when he sees me, they dim slightly. He grabs my hand and tugs me through the crowd to the back storage room. He closes the door and sets a random chair under the handle.

"Are you okay?" he asks, looking me up and down.

I nod, and before I can open my mouth, he shoves me against the wall. He kisses my neck, growling when he inhales and scents the other guy. "You're fucking mine, little bird. No one else can touch you."

I tug him closer so I can rub myself on his thigh, but he steps away with a chuckle. He trails his fingers up the outside of my legs, just under the hem of my skirt, watching every one of my movements. I attempt to move again, to rub myself against him, but he steps away once more. I growl, a pathetic sound compared to his, and he outright laughs.

But his hand slides between my thighs and I whimper with impatience, threading my fingers through his hair. He's moving too slowly, teasing me too much. I shift my hips, doing my best to direct his fingers exactly where I want them.

"Impatient little bird," he mutters, but finally runs his finger through my wetness. A low growl rumbles in his chest and his hips press against my thigh, letting me know he's hard as a fucking rock.

Kai's red rimmed eyes bore into me as he slowly pushes two fingers inside me. He watches my every expression, each breath that falls from my lips, the way my hips move as I chase my pleasure. His thumb grazes my clit and I cry out. The teasing is driving me wild. It's boiling my blood in my veins, and it's not enough.

So I say the words I know will incite both the monster and Kai. I say the words that will give me what I want. "Show me who I belong to," I moan, throwing my head back against the wall.

Kai freezes, his throat works on a swallow and his gaze blazes red for a moment before settling back to gray with the slowly encroaching red. I take matters into my own hands as he stares, and I unbutton his pants, tugging them down. Kai snaps and yanks them out of the way, picking me up and wrapping my legs around his waist at the same time.

His cock rubs against my core and I cling to his neck to give me more leverage as I move my hips, coating his length in my arousal. His strong hands wrap around my waist and lift me, no doubt leaving fingerprint shaped bruises on my flesh. When he lowers me back down, his cock presses against my entrance.

"Yes, Kai. Please," I gasp, trying to wiggle down onto the hardness I want inside of me. "Own me. Destroy me. Possess me."

Kai growls and he tugs me down, sheathing his cock inside me. We both make strangled noises of pleasure, and I go pliant in his arms, letting him do whatever he wants to me. Kai's hips move faster and faster. The fire inside me burns brighter and brighter. The wall against my back is unforgiving but I don't care about the bruises I'll have tomorrow. I just need Kai. And he gives me everything.

When I'm so close to combusting, I tilt my head to the side, silently asking him to bite me. His fangs lengthen and his eyes turn impossibly dark as he watches the pulse flutter in my neck before lowering his mouth to the skin there. My stomach clenches when he presses a gentle kiss to my pulse, so out of context with the dominance and possession he's shown me so far.

He scrapes his fangs along the sensitive skin and I whimper, clenching around him. When his fangs sink in my throat, the pleasure soars through me, lighting me up inside. I come around Kai, my body shaking and shuddering. I can feel each pull he takes on my vein and each one causes my orgasm to crest even higher. I scream his name and I feel his cock thicken before his rhythm turns uneven. He removes his fangs as his body stills, licking up the excess blood.

My head falls to his shoulder and Kai wraps me tightly against him. His heart beats with mine, the same tempo, together. Forever. He doesn't set me down, but he turns around and slides down the wall, keeping me tucked close to him.

"Ellis," he breathes into my hair. "Fuck. I love you so much. It still seems surreal sometimes. Getting to spend time with my beloved, doing things like this, it's just ... I'm the luckiest guy in the world."

I snuggle against him, breathing in his scent. It settles inside me, calming and centering. "I think I win the title of luckiest in the world," I mutter. "You, Cade, and Sterling. All of you guys are mine." I smile against his neck, unable to hold it back. "Yeah. I'm definitely the luckiest."

He chuckles, and the sound vibrates his chest. "We should get back out there before people start to wonder where we are."

"Mmhmm," I say, but I don't move, and neither does he.

"I'm sorry," he says quietly, fingers toying with my curls. "I didn't mean to get so possessive. I saw that guy grab your waist and ... I did my best to keep the monster under control."

"I've told you before. You don't have to apologize for the monster. You both keep me safe and, well, I enjoy the sense of safety. I know I can let my guard down because you guys will always have my back." I shrug, looking into now completely gray eyes. "Plus the sex is always amazing."

He smiles, his face softening with the expression, and he leans forward to gently kiss me. "We'll always protect you, baby girl. You'll always be safe with us."

"I know. Thank you."

We stand and fix our clothes before heading back to the main area of the club. As I walk, Kai's release drips down my thighs, slick and warm. When we get back to the table with Sterling and Cade, my mate's nostrils flare as he scents me. His icy blue eyes darken and he pulls his lower lip between his teeth.

"Are you enjoying your birthday?" Cade asks with a knowing grin.

"Very much so." I hop forward and give Cade a kiss, then Sterling.

"You know," Sterling drawls, "Chloe already left with Cole, and Allie and Connor have been glued together for a while now."

"What are you saying, Sterling?" I ask, tugging on a strand of his silver hair.

"How about we head back to the cabin," he suggests, tugging my skirt down a little bit. "We can keep celebrating. Just the four of us."

My stomach flip flops and I bounce on my toes. "I think that sounds amazing."

Summer

ELLIS

I PULL UP SHARI'S DRIVEWAY IN MY JEEP AND I ALMOST
run my car into the front of the house. Gracie is sitting outside on
the porch, a book in her hands. I hesitate briefly, wondering if I
should bother her or let her be. But she looks up from the book
and smiles at me. My heart stops and I find it hard to breathe for a
moment. Gracie is outside, and she smiled at me.

I hop out of the Jeep and head to the front porch. "Hey," I
say, sitting next to her. "What are you reading?"

She holds out the book for me to see the title. Something
historical. If I were to guess, it's probably the safest subject for her
to read. We lapse into silence, and for the first time, it doesn't
seem awkward. Birds are chirping in the trees surrounding the
house, their song a delightful melody that lifts my spirits. The
wind blows warmly, tugging at the strands of my hair that have
escaped my braid. It's cooler on the porch in the shade, but out in
the sun, the heat is brutal. Summer is in full swing.

"Ellis," Gracie says quietly. "I don't think I ever told you how
happy I am for you."

I glance at her with raised brows, questioning.

"Every time I see you, you seem happier and happier. You're

practically glowing with joy and peace. And I'm really glad you have that. You deserve it."

I open my mouth to say something, but close it again. I'm not sure how to respond to that. I don't want to rub it in or brag about how great my life is. But I also don't want to brush off her words. She's not finished talking, though.

"I also wanted to tell you that I'm sorry."

"Sorry for what?" I blurt, whipping my head in her direction.

"I'm sorry that our relationship is so strained now. We used to be inseparable, and I know you want that back. It's just … it's like I don't know who I am anymore. I'm trying to find myself again, and I don't know if I will be the same person I was when we were younger. And I'm sorry."

I shake my head and take her hand. "Gracie, I don't want you to apologize for that. You have done nothing wrong. Of course I would like our relationship to be like it was when we were younger, but that's not possible anymore. I'm a different person than I was then too. We both are. I know there is no going back to that, and I don't want to go back to that." I squeeze her hand, trying to relay how much I mean these words. "I want us both to be who we are now. And I know it's going to take us time to figure out how our relationship looks after everything we've both been through. So no apologies for that."

She nods and a relieved look crosses her face, her shoulders slumping slightly as they lose the tension she was carrying in them. We fall silent again, gently rocking in the swing, when Cole's truck tears up the driveway.

He gets out, slamming the door and stomps up the steps. "The most infuriating fucking woman I've ever met," he mutters to himself before storming inside.

I smile and pull out my phone, sending a quick text Chloe. *What did you do now?*

She responds back with, *It's not me! It's him! He needs to remember I'm not a wolf, and he can't control me like one.*

I chuckle and show Gracie, and she just shakes her head.

"He's been really mopey lately," she says. "He comes home in a huff and then sulks the rest of the day."

I hum and push to my feet. "I'm going to go talk to Shari real quick. You'll still be out here?"

Gracie nods and I head inside, following the scent of peanut butter and flour to the kitchen. Shari stands at the counter, covered in flour, her hands sticky with something.

"Ellis!" she exclaims, turning around. She stops herself before giving me a hug. "Oh, I'd hug you but I'm covered in peanut butter."

"What are you making?" I glance at the counter and the bowls and ingredients.

"No bake cookies. Or as Sterling and Cole always called them, doggie drips."

My nose crinkles at the descriptive term, but I laugh and snag one from the kitchen table sitting in a tupperware container. "Delicious as always. Have you ever made something gross?"

She laughs and shakes her head. "I learned from my grandmother. She was a perfectionist, and I was too scared to make mistakes."

"Well it paid off," I say, grabbing a second cookie. "Do you have any extras I could take home to the boys?"

"You can take that container. Are you ready for your vacation?"

"Mentally, yes. Physically? Not so much. I still need to pack. And I'm here because I'm putting it off."

"That sounds about right." She returns to the mixing bowl and starts mixing the ingredients with her hands, hence the peanut butter covering them. "I'm assuming you talked with your sister?"

"Yes, I did. I'm really glad to see her outside."

Shari nods. "She's been sitting out there most days the past few weeks. And, she's come downstairs and joined me for dinner a few times. Even one time when Cole was here."

My eyebrows climb to my hairline. "Really? Oh my gosh that

makes me so happy to hear. I know it's not a lot, but it's so big for her."

"It's huge. She's doing a lot better. I've spotted her outside writing in that journal you got her for Christmas. I think it's helping. I keep mentioning therapy, in the hopes I'll wear her down."

"Well, I can't thank you enough for everything you've done for her and for letting her stay. It really means a lot to me." I blink back the tears that burn my eyes. No words will ever be enough to share my gratitude for everything Shari has done. From letting my sister stay here, to helping Cade's mom and sister. Not to mention bringing my mate into the world.

"Oh stop those tears," Shari says, blinking away her own. "You don't need to thank me for anything. I'd say it's what family does, but I know that will just make you cry harder."

I laugh and sniffle at the same time, because she's right. Before I can say anything else though, something crashes upstairs, followed by Cole's cursing. Shari sighs and shakes her head, turning back to her baking.

"Has that been happening a lot?" I wipe my cheeks of the few tears that escaped.

Shari nods. "I don't think he knows how to woo a woman. I don't blame Chloe for holding out, but it's certainly making my life more difficult."

I bite my bottom lip and debate. It's not really my place to get involved, but Chloe is my friend. Cole is known to get a stick up his ass, and last time I was the one to help him pull it out. I grab a cookie from the table and head up to his room.

I knock and wait, but he doesn't answer. "I'm coming in, so you better be dressed. I really don't want to see you naked." Pushing the door open slowly, I peek inside with one eye.

Cole is sitting on the bed, shirtless, but wearing pants. He lifts his gaze to mine, his eyes so similar to Sterling's.

"Bad day?" I ask with an overly saccharine smile.

He glares at me. "I'm assuming you already talked to Chloe?"

When I don't answer he huffs. "Let me guess, you're here to yell at me too?"

I step further into the room to lean against the doorframe. "I'm not here to yell. Believe it or not, I'm rooting for you. That's why I'm here to offer you my advice."

He raises his brows and looks at the cookie in my hand. "Are you going to bribe me with a cookie?"

"Hell no. This is mine." I pop the entire thing in my mouth and grin around the treat.

Cole rolls his eyes and flops back onto his bed like a petulant toddler. "What could you possibly tell me that will make Chloe accept the bond?"

"You need to remember she's not a wolf, Cole," I say around a mouthful of cookie. Swallowing, I continue, "She lived her life, up until the point of her capture, thinking she'd end up with a mage. Mages and wolves are very different. Chloe is strong-willed and spirited. She won't take well to someone bossing her around. And I know how possessive you wolves are. That's not what she needs or wants." I sit on the edge of his bed, watching his face for any kind of reaction. "Not to mention, she spent how long living in a cage under Thomas Kennedy's thumb. She won't tolerate someone telling her what to do or trying to control her life."

"What are you saying, then?"

"Chloe needs someone who will stand by her and support her while she makes her own decisions. I'm not saying to not protect her, because while she may not admit it, she appreciates that. She just doesn't need the alphahole possessiveness that comes with the protection. She needs to be able to live her life how she wants with your support and love."

Cole is silent for a moment, thinking over my words. When he finally speaks, he does so with a frown. "I don't know how to prevent my wolf from being so possessive. It's in my nature."

"Well, you and your wolf need to figure it out. Do you want your mate? Or do you want to lose her to something you could prevent? You can't have both, Cole. You have to choose." I stand from the bed and give him an encouraging smile. "She really does like you. But she won't give up who she is after having lived so long as a nobody in Kennedy's prison."

With that, I leave, pulling the door closed behind me. I hope I got through to him, because I meant what I said. I'm rooting for him. Chloe really does like him, and she wants to accept the bond. But she won't do it if Cole doesn't figure out how to treat her.

"Are you leaving?" Shari calls from the kitchen as I walk downstairs.

"Not yet. I'm going to go sit with Gracie some more."

"Don't forget to say bye before you leave," Shari admonishes.

"Wouldn't dream of it. Besides, I can't leave those cookies behind."

"DO YOU WANT ANOTHER COFFEE?" Cade asks as we make our way through the airport a couple days later.

"Yes, please," I mumble, shuffling along next to them.

I'm trying to keep my focus away from all the people crowded inside the airport this early in the morning. Where could they all possibly be going? This is my first time being at an airport. Whenever we traveled as kids, we used Kennedy's private jet.

I know there is nothing to worry about anymore. And I'm not worried about my safety. With my Shields next to me, I know I'm safe. But a lot of people stare at us. Not only because they recognize Kai, Cade, and Sterling. When they realize I'm *with* all three of them, the stares only get more intense. I try to tell myself not to worry about it, but it's hard. This is the first time we've all been out together during the day and not in a dark club filled with drunk partygoers. I can't help but be paranoid.

The guys seem to sense my unease, because Kai and Cade keep a little separated from me and Sterling, to make it appear like we are two separate couples. I hate that they feel the need to do that because of me, but no matter how I try to ignore it, I can't.

We find our gate and take our seats to wait; me with another coffee thanks to Cade. Sterling and Cade sit on either side of me, and Kai hesitates a moment, looking at me. Biting the bullet, I motion for him to sit on the floor in front of me, between my legs. His smile makes it all worth it. He plops down and rests his head on my thigh.

"So, I've been thinking," I say softly, running my fingers through his hair.

"Uh oh," Kai says, looking up at me with his gray eyes. "That's never good for us."

I smack the back of his head and glare at him. "I don't want to keep Kennedy as my last name. Not only is he not my father, but he's a horrible person. I don't want to be associated with him. However, I obviously can't take all of your last names, and choosing just one doesn't seem right."

"We could draw straws," Kai says, grinning at me. "Or we could just pick the most obvious one. Ellis Thorne. I mean, my last name has the most impact."

Cade snorts. "Right. Like she'd want to take your last name. Besides, Ellis Campbell has a better ring to it."

"You're both pathetic if you think she'd take your name," Sterling grumbles.

Kai raises his brows at Sterling. "Oh, and you think Ellis Harrison sounds good?"

He shrugs. "I'm alpha of the Iron Shadows pack. My name is powerful."

I bite my lip to keep from smiling at their banter. It's unfortunate I can't take all three, but that would be not only illegal, but also a mouthful. *Ellis Thorne Campbell Harrison.* Our children would hate us.

"While I love the idea of taking all of your names, I had another idea." I draw their attention away from their argument of whose last name is best. "What if I use my mom's maiden's name?"

"What was your mom's last name before she married Kennedy?" Cade asks, seeming surprised he doesn't know it already.

"Gray. Tabitha Gray."

Cade's eyes widen. "She was a Gray? I never realized that. The Grays were one of the most prominent mage families for hundreds of years. Second only to the Kennedy's."

I nod. "Yeah, which is why it was arranged for her and Thomas to marry. The Kennedy's and Gray's hoped merging the two bloodlines would create even more powerful mages." I laugh bitterly. "Too bad my mom must have hated Thomas. Enough that she cheated on him. Not once, but twice. And ended up with two children who had no powers."

"Damn," Cade whistles. "I can only imagine the powerhouse those kids would have been. But," he takes my hand and squeezes it. "I think how it turned out was even better. Besides, you're not so powerless after all."

"Ellis Gray," Kai mutters.

Sterling nods. "I like it. And any kids we have can take that last name, too."

I smile, thinking of the possibilities. Thinking of shedding the horrid last name that means nothing to me, and donning one that preserves my mother's legacy. *Ellis Gray.* "Well, then. It's decided."

ELLIS

I CLOSE MY EYES, TIPPING MY HEAD BACK AND LETTING the sun bathe my skin. The salty wind whips strands of my hair around my face. And the sound of crashing waves brings a smile to my lips. I made sure to wake up early enough to see the ocean in the daylight hours. And the perk of that is getting to watch the sunset.

Sand crunches next to me, and I open my eyes to find Sterling sitting in the sand next to my towel. He leans over, resting his hand behind my back and I lean into him, the motion effortless. A year ago, I never would have been able to do that. My body would have locked up. My heart would have frozen. And my lungs would have seized. Now, I don't feel complete unless one of my guys is with me.

"Cade is making you coffee," he murmurs, brushing his lips against my temple.

I hum contentedly, and watch the waves crash on the shore. Silence falls between us, and the sound of the ocean soothes something inside me. When Cade sits on my other side, he hands me an iced coffee, and the three of us watch the sun sink lower to the horizon. The vibrant oranges, pinks, and purple stain the sky and reflect off the water. It's breathtaking, and I've never seen anything quite so beautiful.

"Thank you," I breathe into the silence. Both of the guys look at me, so I continue. "Thank you for everything." I have to swallow past the lump in my throat that forms at the mere thought of everything these guys have done for me. "You guys saved me. You have given me my life back and so much more. I ..."

Cade gently turns my face to his. His violet eyes are beautiful in the sunset. "Never thank us for that, love. We did it gladly, and would do it again." He kisses me softly, and my throat burns with unshed tears.

"You're our entire world, kitten," Sterling says, brushing his fingers down my arm. "We would do anything for you. And we always will."

I look away, not wanting them to see the emotion that bubbles inside me at their words, but I know they know. We're all so in tune with each other, it's impossible to not know.

We watch the rest of the sunset in silence. I only wish Kai was with us, but sunrise and sunset are the hardest on him. When it's almost too dark to see, Sterling helps me to my feet, and we head back inside.

The condo is right on the beach. The large patio doors open to the sand and ocean beyond. The bed—big enough for all of us —is positioned to see the view from the windows. The curtains are closed now, though, to keep the sun out. But with the darkness outside, we leave the doors open and Cade tugs open the curtains.

Kai is laying in the massive bed alone. He's awake but only just barely. He looks at me sleepily, his black hair mussed. I climb into bed with him and snuggle against his side. His arms come around me and hold me tight.

"How's the view?" he asks, voice rough with sleep.

When we arrived it was the middle of the day. We hurried to the condo, and because we're all so used to sleeping at night, we passed out immediately.

"Beautiful," I say, kissing his chest. "The sunset was gorgeous. I wish you could have seen it."

He hums and presses a kiss to the top of my head. "That's okay. I get to see something even more beautiful every day."

A fake gagging noise draws my attention, and I look up to find Cade bending over and pretending to vomit. "So gross," he mutters.

"You're just jealous I said that about Ellis and not you," Kai retorts.

Cade glares at us and walks away, leaving me giggling. "So, what's the plan for today?" I ask snuggling back down with Kai.

"This," he says. "Laying in bed with you."

I think that sounds wonderful. But Cade and Sterling have a different idea. They come back to the bedroom, both of them wearing swim trunks. My gaze snags on their muscled torsos and gets stuck.

Kai prods me in the side. "You're drooling on me."

"Am not," I mutter, but I make sure to close my mouth.

Sterling tosses a bathing suit toward me, and I stare at it sprawled on the bed. "I took it upon myself to buy you a new swimsuit. I'm sure that one piece looked adorable on you, but..."

My cheeks heat and I duck my head against Kai's chest. "Stop making fun of me."

The bed dips as Cade flops down next to Kai, getting in my face. "It was very cute, but this is so much better." He grins, then tugs Kai's head around to kiss him roughly. "You too, loverboy. We're going swimming."

THE BATHING SUIT Sterling picked out fits perfectly. I have no idea how he does it, but he never fails when he buys me clothes. And I always love everything he picks out for me. The top is leopard print with thin adjustable straps. The entire thing ties in between my breasts with a bow. The bottoms are simple black, but they also tie on the sides. I have a feeling those ties will be pulled tonight and the suit removed.

All three guys are already on the beach when I exit the condo. The sand is still warm under my feet from the sun beating down on it all day, but when I dig my toes in deeper, it's cool and wet. It squishes between my toes as I make my way to the guys. There's a large cabana bed on the beach with curtains that can be untied to block the sun. I set my towel on it and put my hands on my hips.

"Does this pass your approval?" I ask, raising one brow.

All three guys stare at me with hungry gazes. Cade steps up to me and wraps his hands around my waist. "Fucking perfect," he mutters against my neck, making my toes curl in the sand.

Kai laughs and wades into the ocean, bracing himself against the waves as they crash against him. He dives under a swell, popping up on the other side and spraying salt water as he shakes his hair from his face.

"Let's go." Sterling takes my hand and tugs me forward.

The water is warm as it swirls around my calves. The current pushes and pulls as the waves crash onto the shore then recede. Sterling sweeps me into his arms and carries me further out into the ocean. I cling to him, hesitant about the dark waters around us, a slight fear of what's swimming around me unknown, making my skin prickle.

"Don't worry," he whispers in my ear, making me shiver for an entirely different reason. "You'll be fine."

He sets me down in waist deep water but keeps his hands on my waist. Behind me I hear a yelp, and I whirl around to see Cade emerge from the water, spluttering and wiping his face.

"Fucking vampire," he growls, searching the dark water. Without any warning, he disappears again, another yelp getting cut off as his head sinks below the surface.

Kai pops up, grinning maniacally, his fangs glinting in the moonlight. A look of pure shock crossing his features as Cade rises from the water, tackling him from behind and pushing his head under.

"Two can play that game," Cade says breathlessly.

I lean back into Sterling's arms and watch Cade and Kai take turns shoving each other underwater. Kai's curses are sharp and imaginative, and I find myself laughing more than I have in a long time. For all Kai's supernatural grace, Cade manages to get the upper hand on him quite a few times.

Sterling's fingers trace idle patterns on my stomach, and his chest rumbles with laughter as we watch the boys. "It's nice finally being able to let our guards down a little bit," he says quietly.

I smile at the 'little bit' comment because I know with them, their guard will never be totally down. "It still seems like a dream to me sometimes. Like I'll wake up and realize none of it's real. It doesn't seem possible I could be allowed this much happiness."

Sterling's arms tighten around me and he kisses my shoulder right where it meets my neck. "It's not a dream, kitten. And you deserve all of the happiness and then some. And we'll do everything in our power to keep it that way."

Cade jumps on Kai's back, and Kai somehow manages to keep his balance and not be pushed under. Maybe he was letting Cade win all those times. The thought makes me giggle, almost as much as the way the tension between the two of them sparks to life. Cade's grip around Kai's chest loosens, his hands trailing over Kai's smooth skin while his head drops to Kai's neck.

Heat builds in my belly, and Sterling clearly senses the shift in me. He nips at my earlobe, growling low in his chest. "Are you watching them, kitten?" His fingers dip into the waist of my bikini bottom.

"Yes," I breathe, eyes glued to my two guys.

"Tell me what you see."

I open my mouth to say something, but his finger slides to my core, and a gasp escapes my lips. He pauses, clearly waiting for me to speak before doing anything else. "I see Cade kissing Kai's neck." The finger moves lower, gathering my arousal and sliding back up to my clit, then pausing. "Cade's hand is in Kai's pant—" I break off with a gasp as Sterling's finger circles my clit.

"Don't stop," he growls.

"Kai's head is … is tipped back and … and he's biting his bottom lip."

Sterling's finger flicks over my clit making me whimper and my hips jerk. I lose my train of thought as every bit of my focus narrows to what he's doing to me. At least until he stops, waiting expectantly for me to continue.

"Cade is in front of Kai now, and … and. Fuck, Sterling," I breathe, rolling my hips as he slips two fingers inside of me.

Sterling growls, the sound vibrating against my back. "I'm pretty sure I'm not there, kitten. Keep describing what they're doing."

I suck in a breath and try to clear my head, but it's impossible with Sterling fucking me with his fingers. "They're kissing, and oh gods, it's so hot." I grab Sterling's wrist and try to rub the heel of his hand against my clit, but he's too strong.

"Do you want to be in the middle of them?" he asks, voice low and seductive. His breath fans over my neck a second before he licks up the side of my throat. "Do you want them to worship you while they fuck each other?"

I whimper at the picture his words conjure in my mind. Being in the middle of them, with Sterling giving orders and letting all of us be able to just let go, is something I will never, ever, get tired of.

"That's not an answer, kitten." He bites my earlobe making my core clench around his fingers. He chuckles darkly and withdraws from my body before bringing his fingers to his mouth and sucking my pleasure from them. A low growl rumbles in his chest. "Call them to you. Let them know you want them."

I call Kai's name first, because with his supernatural hearing, I know he'll hear me. But my voice is breathy and it doesn't carry far enough. Without warning, Sterling pinches my nipple through my swimsuit top, and I gasp loudly. That get's Kai's attention and he snaps his head in my direction. He mutters something to Cade and they both grin before wading to me.

Kai grabs me around the waist and throws me over his shoulder, smacking my ass hard and making me squeal. With my hands on his low back, I push my head up and look at Cade and Sterling as they follow us to the shore. Their gazes are dark and glued to me, desire obvious in their expressions. Just seeing how much they want me makes me crave them even more. I love having this kind of power over such badass men. Knowing they can kill someone in the blink of an eye, yet worship me with those same bloody hands is exhilarating.

The world spins as Kai drops me, and my stomach rises to my throat until I crash onto the cabana bed. All three guys stand over me as I scoot back, slowly discarding their bathing suits, and the sight makes my mouth water and my core heat.

Kai looks at Sterling with an expectant raised brow, his piercing catching the light from the moon. "What would you have us do?" His voice is low and dark, promising wicked things to come.

Sterling's smile is just as wicked. "Make her squirm."

ELLIS

Cade and Kai descend on me and my breath catches in my throat. Their fingers trace over my skin, teasing and slowly stoking the flames inside me. I let my hands trail over their bodies, Kai's cooler to the touch than Cade's. When my gaze snags against Cade's, he lowers his head and kisses me. It's not his usual sweet kiss that slowly drugs me into oblivion. It's commanding and rough like he's having a hard time controlling himself. It's been like that with him since I had my implant removed.

Kai snags the tie between my breasts in his teeth, and he tugs it until it unravels. Slowly, he teases the top apart, making sure the fabric scrapes against my sensitive nipples. His teeth replace the fabric, fangs gently biting and sending electricity straight to my core.

"Someone," I gasp, "Please touch me." My legs are pressed together as I desperately attempt to ease the ache between them.

Kai releases my nipple and trails nips and kisses down my ribs and stomach. He slowly pulls my bathing suit bottom down my legs and tosses it to the ground. Cade replaces Kai, sucking my other nipple into his mouth and pinching the one Kai just released. My back arches off the bed and I let my legs fall open in a silent plea to them to touch me where I need it most.

Kai growls as he lowers his head to my core, inhaling my scent but not touching me. I try to reach down to push his head against me, but Cade grabs my hands and pins them above my head. His magic slithers over my skin in a sensual warmth, bright purple light casting all of us in a violet glow. It settles around my wrists, binding my hands above my head and pinning them to the cabana bed. There is no fear. No trepidation at being restrained by magic. My Shields have wiped that part of my past from my body with their never-ending love and patience.

Kai's finger trails through my core, gathering my arousal on his finger. "You are so fucking ready for us, baby girl." He licks his finger, eyes closing as if he's tasting the most delicious delicacy. Then he lowers down to lick straight from the source.

A moan climbs up my throat and falls from my lips. Between Cade's teeth and fingers on my nipples, and Kai's tongue on my core, they make me squirm just as Sterling demanded. I force my eyes open to look at my alpha, and I almost lose it at the sight of him naked with his hard cock in hand, stroking slowly as he watches us.

He grins at me and walks around the cabana bed to sit on the side. "Kai, you're first. But don't let her come."

My body lights up at his command. There is a wicked promise in his icy blue eyes, and I know they are going to shove me to the edge over and over again until I break. And when I break, it will be the most beautiful thing ever.

Kai never takes his eyes off me as he takes himself in hand and rubs the tip of his cock up and down my core. I can't keep my hips from lifting, searching for more. But when he presses the head of his cock against my entrance, I still. He holds my gaze as he slowly pushes inside, filling and stretching me deliciously.

"Kai," I gasp, my fingers opening and closing above my head.

When he's seated fully, he leans over with hands on either side of my head and gently kisses me. "Are you ready, baby girl?" he whispers against my mouth. "Remember, you can't come." His fang catches my lip and a bead of blood forms. Kai grins as he licks it away.

When he pulls out, I whimper at the loss of him, but he gives me no time to mourn. His hips slam into mine and a cry falls from my lips. He sets a relentless pace and the entire time he holds my gaze. His gray eyes are shining in the moonlight, making him look almost feral. It's incredibly sexy.

Kai's fingers dig sharply into my hips, and then he pulls out. He flips me over and lifts my ass into the air. With my hands bound, I can't support myself. But as Kai slides back inside, he grabs a fistful of my hair and yanks me up. The pain in my scalp shoots like lightning to my core and I clench around Kai.

"Not yet, baby girl," he growls, sliding one hand to my throat and the other to my hip. "Sterling didn't say you could come." Then he pistons his hips faster and faster. His hand around my throat tightens and he leans down to drag his fangs over my neck.

I whimper, but he doesn't bite me. And it's probably a good thing. If he did, I would have come apart immediately. As it is, my blood is boiling. Kai's rough fucking is brining me higher and higher. But he doesn't let me fall over the edge. His body stiffens behind me and his thrusting stutters. He spills himself inside me with a soft grunt, his cock pulsing until he pulls out.

Kai gently rolls me over onto my back and kisses me. It's sweet and so different from how he just fucked me. His release is warm as it slides between my thighs and his eyes light up knowing exactly what I just thought.

"Cade," Sterling says, his voice like gravel and strained. "You're next." I glance at Sterling. His cock is straining. Liquid beads at the tip and I lick my lips, wanting to taste it. He shakes his head with a smirk. "Not tonight, Kitten. I want you to ride Cade now."

Cade lies down on his back and I try to climb on top of him. It's difficult with my hands bound, but he lifts me and settles me against his cock. We both groan as I roll my hips, slicking his cock in Kai's release. When he realizes Kai's cum is still dripping down my thighs, it seems to light a fire in him. He lifts me up and I slide onto his cock easily, resting my bound hands on his chest for support. I settle into a rhythm, and Cade lays back with his hands on my hips and watches me ride him through lowered lids.

"That's it, love," he says. "Don't stop."

I didn't plan on it, but the more I roll my hips the harder it gets to keep myself from tipping over the edge. I need to come so bad, and each roll of my hips hits that spot inside of me that makes me see stars. I bite my lip hard enough to draw blood in an attempt to distract myself.

A whimper climbs up my throat at the same time my hips stutter. Cade grabs them and lifts his own hips to slam into me. He does this again and again, each time bringing me closer to exploding. But right before I can, he pulls me down on top of him and he holds me tightly as his body shudders through his release. His hot breath on my neck makes me shiver, and when he finally stills, he kisses the spot just below my ear.

Cade rolls me over onto my back and pulls out. Filled with his and Kai's releases, I feel it sliding out of me. Cade watches it with a fire in his eyes that lights me up. He swallows thickly and moves to the side, sitting next to Kai.

Then Sterling leans over me, careful to not touch me. "Do you know how beautiful you look, kitten? When you're flushed with desire and wild with sex?" His gaze slides over my body, stopping between my spread thighs. He growls and I feel it rumble the bed beneath me. "So fucking beautiful filled with my brothers' releases and waiting for mine."

I whimper. "Please, Sterling. I need to come." It's almost painful how badly I need it.

"Patience, kitten. I'll let you come in just a minute." He runs his hands over my breasts, stopping to pinch my nipples, then over my ribs to my thighs. He grips them tightly and spreads me wide, kneeling between them. "Are you ready, kitten?"

He doesn't wait for an answer. Instead he slams into me.

There is no resistance. Between my own arousal and both Kai and Cade's releases, he slides right in. I cry out as he fills me. And he doesn't give me a chance to suck in another breath. Sterling crushes his mouth to mine and I greedily meet his tongue with my own.

I wish my hands were free. I want to run them through his silver hair and tangle my fingers in the strands. I want to trace over every inch of his body, already slick with sweat. But being restrained, even just my hands, is one more thing that drives me higher and higher. Left to their mercy and given a sense of being defenseless.

Noises to my right draw my gaze, and I almost lose it right then. Kai and Cade are hard again, pressed against each other with both of their cocks in Cade's hand. I have to squeeze my eyes shut and suck in a breath. I'm so fucking close, and I don't think I can hold on any longer.

"Please, Sterling," I rasp. "Please, let me come."

He growls, dropping his mouth to my mating mark. "Almost, kitten. Just hold on a little bit more. I know you can." His tongue trails over my mark, and I shiver, clenching around him. "Oh, fuck," he growls. "Kai," he bites out through clenched teeth.

Without any further instruction, Kai leans over and sinks his fangs into my neck. At the same time, Cade's magic slides over my stomach, through my core, and wraps around my clit. My scream is torn from my throat as my body combusts. Pleasure like I've never experienced roars through me. With Kai's fangs, Cade's magic, and Sterling's cock, my body practically convulses as the waves of pleasure crash through me again and again.

As my body comes down, I'm aware of Sterling's nose buried in my neck as he shudders above me. And Cade and Kai are both groaning, like they came as well. But my body is too limp to move. My eyes won't open. With each thump of my heart racing in my chest, I'm one step closer to completely passing out.

Sterling pulls away, but doesn't go far. He settles next to me, and places his hand low on my belly. "I'm going to sleep well tonight, knowing you're filled to the brim with our cum." His voice is low and quiet, and it makes me shiver. His words and hand placement making my stomach tumble. This night was planned for a very specific reason.

Cade settles on my other side. "Sleep, love. We'll be here." He kisses my shoulder and places his hand just above Sterlings.

"You did great, baby girl. Fucking perfect." Kai leans over Cade and kisses me gently, then threads his fingers through Cade's on my stomach.

I smile sleepily, unable to form any words, and I snuggle against them, letting sleep pull me under.

WHEN I WAKE, the guys are still asleep around me. My head is on Cade's chest with Sterling's arm around my waist. I blink the sleep away and listen to the sound of the waves crashing against the shore while I watch Kai sleep. The ocean breeze tugs strands of his black hair this way and that, and his dark lashes fan across his pale cheeks.

I realize the sky is lightening enough for me to see his features, and I sit up quickly, looking out over the ocean. The sun is rising above the horizon, the first rays piercing the darkness and painting the sky a vibrant shade of pink. As beautiful as it is, I don't keep my gaze on it long.

"Kai," I say, reaching over Cade to shake the vampire awake. "Kai, the sun is coming up."

His gray eyes open, squinting at the light that probably burns them. Sitting up and stretching with his arms over his head, he grins at me. "That's okay. I want to watch the sun rise with you."

"Are you sure?" My gaze travels over his pale naked body, covered in black tats.

He nods and reaches out a hand for me. I climb over Cade,

accidentally kneeing him in the stomach. Cringing, I settle between Kai's legs with my back against his chest.

"What the fuck?" Cade groans, doubling over and clutching his stomach.

"Sorry," I whisper, ducking my head and trying to make myself look as innocent as possible.

He grunts and sits up, eyeing me sideways. "Nice try, love. That innocent look doesn't work on you."

"Are we going to watch Kai burn to a crisp this morning?" Sterling asks through a yawn, joining the rest of us leaning against the head of the cabana bed.

"Vampire toast. It's what's for breakfast." Cade grins, elbowing Kai in the ribs.

Sterling makes a noise in the back of his throat. "I'll pass. Too scrawny."

"Fuck off, both of you." Kai tightens his arms around my waist, and hooks his chin over my shoulder. "I can't stand them," he mumbles.

I giggle, letting their antics wash over me as I watch the sky turn orange then yellow. Waking up naked on the beach with my guys, the sound of the waves and the scent of the ocean, it's a memory I'll cherish for the rest of my life. I shift in Kai's arms and smile. The soreness between my legs reminds me of what happened last night. With Kai's hand on my belly, I can't help but wonder if last night will be the night that changes our lives forever.

"Who's up for a morning swim?" Cade asks before leaning over and kissing Kai thoroughly before giving me the same treatment. He doesn't wait for an answer before stepping onto the sand and dashing for the ocean.

Luckily the beach is private, so I don't have to worry about someone seeing my guys naked, because that would seriously ruin my good mood. Sterling grins at me and gives me a quick kiss before following Cade.

"You gonna join them?" Kai asks, reaching over to pull the

curtains closed on both sides, leaving the front open to the view of Cade and Sterling in the ocean.

"No, not right now. I'm enjoying sitting here with you."

Kai's chest rumbles against my back, and he tucks me closer to him. "Good. Because I'm enjoying it too." He kisses my neck, on the bite mark there that signifies I'm his. It sends a wave of heat through me, and I tilt my head to the side in invitation. He chuckles darkly. "If I bite you," he says, his breath warm on my neck, "you know Cade and Sterling won't last long in the water before they have to join us."

"And that would be such a shame," I murmur, gripping his thighs tightly in my hands.

"It really would." His tongue licks up the side of my neck, and I shiver as pleasure runs down my spine. "Too bad for them, I'm ready for my breakfast."

Autumn

ELLIS

Leaves crunch under my boots as I walk to the porch, bags hanging from my hands. A crisp breeze blows my curls away from my face, and I inhale the scent of autumn. Cade bought pumpkins for all of us the other day, and they sit on the stairs awaiting their time to be carved. This is probably my favorite time of year. When the leaves change colors and fall from the trees. When the temperature turns chilly enough to need a hoodie. And the nights are perfect for bonfires and beers.

Inside, I catch a whiff of pumpkin spice and cinnamon, and I head to the kitchen. Kai is at the stove, pulling a tray of something from the oven, a pale pink apron wrapped around him.

"Do I want to know what you're making?" I ask, setting my bags on the table before going to his side.

He shoots me a glare and drops the oven mitts on the counter. "Pumpkin cookies, for Shari's party tomorrow. And before you ask, yes, they are safe to eat." He frowns and sets his hands on his hips. "I think."

"Well, let's wait for Cade to get home before anyone tries them." I grin at his disgruntled look and wrap my arms around him, turning him to face me. "It's just a precaution. We don't need anyone dying over a cookie."

Although Kai has been doing pretty good with his baking, cooking is another matter entirely. Baking he seems to be getting the hang of. He mutters something under his breath that I choose to ignore. I take a breath and frown. Usually I like the smell of pumpkin spice, but for some reason, it's just not doing it for me right now.

"Come on," I say, taking his hand in one of mine, while grabbing the bags from the table in my other. "I have something to show you." I lead Kai to the living room and push him onto the couch, holding out my shopping bags. "I did some shopping today, and I may have stopped by a costume store."

"Oh no," he groans. "Please tell me you didn't buy us costumes for the party tomorrow."

I grin and reach into the first bag, pulling out Sterling's costume. Kai chokes and has to thump himself on the chest.

"Is that ..." he trails off in a fit of laughter, actually snorting once before he gets himself under control. "A dog warden costume. Seriously fucking hilarious."

"I thought so," I grin and put it back, taking out Cade's. "A Prince Charming costume. Because Cade is my prince charming."

Kai smiles and nods. "Mine too." We share a look before he asks, "What about my costume?"

I grin and hold up his, watching his face closely for his reaction. His smile drops, and he glares at me.

"Seriously, Ellis? A fucking hotdog?"

A laugh bursts from me so hard I double over. "I thought .. it ... was perfect," I say between breaths.

"I don't even eat hotdogs!" He grabs the costume from me and holds it up, frowning.

"You eat Cade's." I can't stop the words from leaving my mouth, and Kai's gaze snaps to mine. I give him a cheeky grin and raise one brow, daring him to deny it.

He tosses the costume to the side and stands in a rush. "You little brat," he growls, grabbing me around the waist and throwing me over his shoulder.

I shriek and laugh as he takes me upstairs and dumps me on the bed. "Wait," I manage to say before he does anything else. "I need to shower. I worked out today at the gym. I'm gross."

"I don't care," he says darkly.

"Yeah, but I do. Just give me two minutes." I jump from the bed and head to the bathroom, taking my clothes off as I go.

Kai lasts three minutes before he storms into the bathroom and joins me in the shower. "You're taking too long," he growls, shoving me against the wall and claiming my mouth.

I melt instantly. My fingers tangle in his rapidly dampening hair and I roll my hips against his. The past couple of days I've been incredibly horny, and it's almost like I can't get enough of my guys. Kai lifts me, wrapping my legs around his waist and he presses his cock against my entrance. Pleas fall from my lips as he teases me, running those wicked fangs over my throat. And when he decides he's had enough teasing, he thrusts inside roughly.

I scream and cling to him, letting him completely fill me. It doesn't take me long to get off. My body seems like it's always primed for them the past few days. When the shaking stops, Kai shuts off the water, forgoing the actual washing, and walks me to the bed, never pulling out of me.

The sensation of him inside me while walking fans the flames that the first orgasm didn't quench. When he lays me on the bed, propped above me, I tilt my neck, needing the pure euphoria his bite brings. With a feral grin, Kai sinks his fangs into my throat, and the first waves of my orgasm crash through me. I don't even notice when Kai quickly pulls away.

It isn't until my orgasm passes that I realize he is staring at me with wide, disbelieving eyes. "What?" I ask between breaths.

He shakes his head, brow pulled down over his eyes, and he leans in to lick at the puncture marks. Normally that action would course through me, but something about Kai's expression has cooled my lust. When he pulls back again, a drop of my blood on his lips, his gray eyes swim with emotion I can't name.

"Ellis," he breathes, cupping my cheek gently.

"Kai, you're scaring me." I try to sit up, but he keeps me where I am. All traces of desire have fled, like having a bucket of cold water dumped on me.

He licks the drop of blood, closing his eyes, and a slow smile spreads across his face. "Ellis, you're pregnant."

"Wh-what?" I gasp, squirming out from under him to sit up.

He grins at me, placing his hand on my belly, and his eyes line with blood. The first time I saw Kai cry, I freaked out. I never realized vampires cry blood. Even knowing that now, it doesn't make it any less unsettling as a single bloody tear slips down his cheek.

"I can taste it, the change in your blood," he says quietly. "You're pregnant, baby girl."

I stare at him. Unable to process his words. My hands drift to my stomach, and I place them over his. It makes sense. I've been feeling off the past couple of days, queasy in the morning, horny *all* the time. And food and scents I usually enjoy have turned my stomach. My periods have never been consistent, and when I removed my implant, they went right back to being all out of whack. So I never even thought twice about my period being late.

"Pregnant?" I ask, eyes blurring with tears.

Kai nods, his smile spreading even wider before wrapping me in his arms and holding me tight. "We're going to have a baby, Ellis," he breathes.

Those words freeze me, and I pull back sharply, placing my hands over my mouth. "But ..."

He frowns, taking my hands in his. "What? I thought you wanted this?" He searches my face, the one bloody tear track stained on his cheek.

"I do. I really do, but ..." I swallow and look away from him. "What if it's not yours?"

He laughs, and I snap my gaze to him again. "Ellis, baby girl, I thought all of our discussions about starting a family made it clear. I don't fucking care whose baby it is. That child is mine."

He places his hand on my stomach again, and stares at me so intently I can't break his stare. "He or she is mine to protect and love, and I will raise them as if they are my flesh and blood."

My tears spill over, and I cover his hand on my stomach. I know that's what they all said when we discussed this. But in the moment, I had a surge of fear he would change his mind. To hear his reassurance opens a dam inside me. I'm going to be a mother. We are going to have a baby.

Kai pulls me against him. "This is everything I've ever dreamed of," he says quietly, running his hands up and down my back. "I am so fucking excited to start this phase with you, baby girl. But ..."

He pulls away and I look at him, my stomach dropping in fear. "But what?" I whisper hoarsely, mentally preparing myself for the worst.

"But I'm going to need you to be patient with me. When a vampire's beloved is with child, they can't drink from them. I won't be able to feed from you. It's too dangerous to the child. Luckily, I have Cade, but it's not quite the same." His gray eyes bounce back and forth as he studies my expression. "Typically, male vampires will get violent as hunger takes over. We get jealous easily, and become very possessive and protective. The need to keep our beloved and child safe becomes our entire focus." He cups my cheek, rubbing his thumb along my cheekbone. "So I'll need you to be patient with me. Like I said, it shouldn't be as bad for me, since I have Cade, but just so you know."

I lean forward and kiss him. "I'll always be patient with you, Kai." Just the thought of having his protection while I'm pregnant eases some anxiety within me. Knowing this child will be loved and cared for makes my heart swell. Then, it sinks. "I guess I need to tell the others."

"Don't worry, baby girl. I can sense that uneasiness inside of you." Kai tucks a curl behind my ear and kisses my forehead. "We're all in this together. We're a family, and they are going to be just as thrilled as I am. Besides, you won't have to tell Sterling. He should be able to scent the change in you any day now. Cade on the other hand, you'll have to tell. He won't be able to tell unless he uses his magic to heal you for something."

I release a breath, looking at my vampire closely. "So this is really happening? I'm really pregnant?"

He smiles wide, fangs on displays. "Yes. We're really having a baby."

A baby. I close my eyes and let it sink in. A family. With my guys. It's really happening.

I SIT in the clinic on the table, the paper wrinkling under me, and chew on my nail. As soon as the clinic opened, I was here, calling Allie to come talk to me. I made sure Cade wasn't here, because I'm not quite ready to tell him. I need the proof.

Allie steps in the room with a smile. "You're pregnant!" She holds out the test results to show me, knowing I'll need to see it with my own eyes.

"Holy shit," I breathe, taking the results with shaking fingers. "I'm really pregnant. Kai was right." I meet Allie's shining eyes and blink back my tears.

"Congratulations," she says, wrapping me in a hug. "El, I am so happy for you."

"I'm going to be so fat for your wedding," I huff, wiping my tears.

"Psh. You're going to be a fucking goddess, girl."

"I can't believe it." I shake my head, pressing my hands against my belly. "I mean, I was trying so hard to not get my hopes up. And I guess I probably should still be cautious, right? How far along am I?"

"If I had to guess, three months. It's hard to know for sure until we do an ultrasound, but since Kai could tell by your blood, and Sterling still hasn't noticed, you have to be close to three months. I'm assuming you want to wait to do an ultrasound until the guys are all with you?"

I nod while mentally doing the math. Three months ago we were on the beach, and Sterling made it perfectly clear that night we all slept together what he was trying to do. Oh gods, it worked. "I guess there is no way to tell whose baby it is?"

Allie shook her head. "You could do an amnio, but I wouldn't recommend it unless its absolutely necessary. I think we'll be able to make an educated guess based on how your pregnancy goes."

"What do you mean?"

"Well, if it's Kai's, it's not going to be an easy pregnancy. Vampire pregnancies are rough. The baby takes a lot from the mother, and it can be dangerous. We'll have to keep an eye on you to make sure you're staying healthy." She squeezes my hands encouragingly as fear settles in my stomach like a stone. "If it's Sterling's or Cade's, you'll probably have a fairly easy pregnancy. Shifter's, especially wolves, are strong, healthy babies. It's honestly most likely Sterling's. Although, with your Harpy blood, who knows."

"I mean, it doesn't really matter in the end. At least in terms of who the dad is. I think, I *hope*, they are all accepting."

Allie snorts. "Girl, I have never met three guys who are so willing to share their woman. I don't see why they wouldn't share their children."

"I just don't want any of them getting upset if they don't have a child of their own, you know? I'm worried it will eventually lead to problems."

"I get it, but honestly, I don't think you have to worry about that." She smiles at me, and helps me down from the table. "Those guys are so incredibly in love with you. And I just know they'll be just as in love with any babies you bring into this world."

I hold her words close to my heart as I leave the clinic and walk to my car. I'll have to talk to the guys about it later. Right now, I have to go home to get ready for the Halloween party tonight on pack lands.

ELLIS

"I'm not wearing it." Kai leans against the bathroom door frame while I fix my hair and do my makeup. He crosses his arms and stares me down, the hotdog costume discarded on the floor behind him.

I set my blush on the counter and turn to face him, sporting a truly fantastic pouty lower lip. "Really? It took me forever to think of a perfect costume for you." Dipping my head down, I look up at him through my lashes.

"That's fucking cheating," he says pointing a finger at me. I take a step closer to him, keeping my pout, and he sighs, reaching out to snag my wrist and pull me against his chest. "It's not fair you can do that and all three of us would do whatever the fuck you asked. Run naked through the streets? No problem. Rob a bank? Done. Kill a fucking unicorn? Just tell us when."

I smile and rest my chin on his chest looking up at him. "I would never abuse such an important power."

He snorts, hand resting on my hips. "What the hell do you call this? Forcing me to wear a fucking hotdog costume."

"It's called keeping me happy."

Shaking his head he grins at me. "Nice way to play it, baby girl." Kai kisses me before pulling away and dropping to his knees.

"You better not be as manipulative as your mother," he murmurs to my stomach before kissing it.

I thread my fingers through his hair, biting my lower lip to keep my smile from spreading across my face. Kai has been so amazingly adoring since he found out I was pregnant. It's been nice having this just between the two of us for the time being. I'll tell Sterling and Cade soon, but right now, it's just me and Kai.

Kai stands and grabs the costume from the floor before giving me one last glare and leaving the room to let me get ready. As I put on my finishing touches and slip into my costume, I hear the guys' laughter downstairs. Or at least, I hear Cade and Sterling's laughter. Kai's curses float upstairs, no doubt giving them a piece of his mind at their comments on his hotdog.

Looking in the mirror, I put on the black hooded robe with pink satin trim and adjust it. The short tiny shorts are also trimmed in pink satin, and a black sports bra completes the look. With my knee high black heeled boots and a pair of pink boxing gloves, I look every inch the sexy boxer. Grinning to myself, I head downstairs.

The guys all stop what they're doing when I step into the living room. Cade looks dashing in his prince costume, and Sterling looks adorable in his dog warden costume. Kai just looks ridiculous, and I can't stop myself from laughing. Dressed as a hotdog, complete with bun and streaks of ketchup and mustard, it's the best thing I've seen all year.

"Kai!" I bend over, holding my stomach as the laughter brings tears to my eyes.

"Yeah, yeah, Keep laughing, baby girl. I'll make you pay for it later."

"Don't make promises you can't keep," I say, straightening and wiping the tears from my cheeks. "You two both look great," I say looking Cade and Sterling over.

"You do, too," Sterling says appreciatively, taking in my costume. "That's perfect for you."

Kai snorts, but walks past me, brushing his fingers subtly over my stomach. Our gazes meet, and the adoration in his gray eyes almost knocks me to my knees.

"Alright, let's go. Kai grab the cookies," Cade reminds the vampire before heading outside.

The crisp autumn air makes my skin pimple, and I pull the robe around me, not that the cheap fabric does much to block the wind. We pile into the Hummer, and I cuddle next to Cade to steal his warmth while Kai drives us to Shari's house where we will meet up for dinner before heading to the pack party.

Halloween is one of the pack's favorite holidays. They gather in the large field on pack land and light a massive bonfire. There's drinking, dancing, and trick-or-treating for the pups. Since Sterling is alpha, and I'm his mate, we're expected to be there, which is why I bought us all costumes.

When we get to Shari's house, we climb out and head inside. As always, her home smells like roasted meats and veggies, and the sweet scent of baked goods. Unfortunately, that sweet scent is pumpkin spice, and I swallow as saliva pools in my mouth while my stomach churns threateningly. Just one of the smells that pregnancy has turned against me.

"Look at you guys!" Shari calls as we step inside. She pulls me in for a hug, then gives the guys hugs as well, with a kiss on the cheek for Sterling. "I love those costumes. Kai, that is perfect."

Kai grumbles under his breath and pinches my ass, making me laugh. I step into the living room and smile. Chloe and Cole are sitting next to each other with Cole's arm around her shoulders. It makes me incredibly happy to see the two of them together, finally.

"Nice, Malakai," Cole grunts, fighting a smile. Cole is dressed as a prisoner in a black and white striped one-piece, while Chloe is dressed as a sexy police officer.

"You look so cute, Chloe!" I rush over to her and she jumps up, giving me a hug.

"Thanks, so do you. Grace is the kitchen."

My heart stops but I dart into the kitchen to see my sister.

She's pulling a tray from the oven, and the fresh scent of pumpkin spice hits my nostrils, making me gag. I dart to the garbage can and clutch my stomach as I heave everything I ate today.

"Ellis! Are you okay?" Gracie is at my side in an instant, rubbing my back and pulling my curls from my face.

When my stomach finally settles, I stand up and wipe my mouth, grimacing. "I'm fine." I grab a glass of water to rinse my mouth and turn to face her. Before I say anything, I make sure no one is around to hear me. Laughter drifts to the kitchen from the living room, and I pull Gracie closer, lowering my voice. "You're going to be an aunt," I say, smiling and placing my hand on my lower belly.

Gracie's light brown eyes go wide and her mouth falls open. "Seriously?"

I nod my head and barely have time to brace myself before she throws herself into my arms.

"Ellis, that is so amazing!" When she pulls back, tears line her eyes, but they don't fall. "I am so happy for you. Do you know who …?"

"No. But it doesn't really matter in the end. And only Kai knows right now, so don't say anything."

"I won't." She smiles broadly and squeaks quietly. "I am so excited to be an aunt."

There's a sparkle in her eyes that makes my heart soar. I hope this gives her a purpose and helps to give her the final boost back into the land of the living. Gracie has been doing great. She's comfortable with the guys that typically come to Shari's house, and she's eating better. But getting her to leave the house is a different matter. Maybe a little niece or nephew will be what it takes to get Gracie over this last hurdle.

I leave Gracie to whatever she's doing in the kitchen, and hop into the little bathroom in the hallway. A quick search under the sink provides me with a toothbrush and toothpaste. With a fresh minty mouth, I leave the bathroom, only to run right into Sterling.

"Oh shit," I say, placing my hand on my heart, feeling it thump wildly in my chest. "You scared me."

He chuckles, icy blue eyes glittering. "Sorry, kitten. That wasn't my intent." He studies me, gaze traveling over my body, and a slight frown pulls his brows down. "Are you okay?"

"Yeah, I'm fine. Why?" I swipe my curls over my shoulder and give him a confident smile.

He cups my cheek, rubbing his thumb just under my lower lip. "You're pale. Are you sure you're okay?"

"I'm positive." But I step into him, wrapping my arms around his waist and inhaling his pine and snow scent, letting it wash the pumpkin spice from my nose. Instantly, my stomach settles.

Sterling's arms come around me, and he kisses the top of my head. As close as I am to him, I sense the miniscule shift in his body. The way his muscles tense and his breath hitches in his lungs. He pulls away far enough to tilt my head to the side and he buries his nose in my neck, inhaling deeply.

When he looks at me, I know he knows. Those icy blue eyes are wide and filled with wonder. He goes back in for another inhale, and soft rumble echoes in his chest. "Ellis," he breathes, looking back at me.

I smile tentatively and nod, taking his hands and placing them on my still flat belly. Sterling goes still, even his breaths stop in his chest. I have no warning when he grabs my ass and lifts me, wrapping my legs around his waist. We're out the back door and across the open field in seconds. The woods surround us in darkness. The moon barely visible behind the passing clouds.

Sterling sinks to the ground, leaves crunching under him as he leans against a large tree. Now his chest is heaving with his breaths, and I can feel the pulse in his neck beating like a jack rabbit under my hand.

"It's true?" he asks, voice quiet and filled with so much emotion it almost gets stuck in his throat.

"It's true," I whisper, taking his face in my palms. "You're going to be a daddy, Sterling."

His lips wobble, and he presses them tightly together to hide it. But he can't stop the tears that fill his eyes from spilling over. Sterling pulls me tight to his chest and he buries his face in my neck. His shoulders shake as he cries, and I hold him back just as tightly. My fingers run through his silver hair, combing out the tangles and giving him the touch I know he needs right now.

When he finally stills, he pulls away, and the sight of him almost makes me cry. He looks wrecked in the best possible way. Disbelief, amazement, love, pure joy. It all shows on his face and in his shining eyes. He stares at me for a moment, and I give him the time he needs to find the words he wants to say.

"I can't believe it," he says after a moment of silence where the only sounds are the wind and the bare branches cracking together. "Since the first moment I found you, the first moment I knew you were my mate and realized we would never be together, I mourned the loss of you. Of everything that we could have been and everything we could have had. I'd given up on every dream I had of having a family." His voice catches, and he swallows, shaking his head. "Ellis, this is a dream I never thought I'd get to experience."

This time, it's my eyes that burn and fill with tears. I blink rapidly to clear my vision. Gently, I wipe his cheeks before giving him a soft kiss. "It's not a dream anymore, Sterling. It's real. And you are going to get that family you deserve. It might look a little different than you initially imagined, but it's *our* family."

He laughs quietly. "It's better than I ever could have imagined. I wouldn't want to do this any other way than raising a child with you, Cade, and Kai. Thank you, Ellis. For giving this to me."

I shake my head, tears tracking down my cheeks. "It should be me thanking you. All of you. Because I wouldn't be here if it weren't for you three. And I know this child will be so incredibly loved. He or she is one lucky baby to have all three of you in their life."

Sterling kisses me. It's gentle and sweet, conveying every

emotion and every thought he has that he can't put into words. It sears me to my marrow, making my stomach flutter and heart skip beats. I know how much this man loves me, but this kiss just proves it even more. And to picture him as a father, doting on our child and loving them as much as he loves me—if not more—it makes my heart hurt in the most beautiful of ways.

"I love you so much, Sterling," I whisper against his mouth.

"Fuck, kitten. You have no idea." His voice is more of a growl, and his fingers tighten on my hips.

I thread my fingers through his hair, tugging on the strands to let him know I want more than this kiss. I want to celebrate this with him, to reinforce and remind him that he's not alone anymore. That he has me, and now this baby. It's a reminder I think he needs every now and then.

Sterling drops his head to my neck and he licks his mark before gently pressing his teeth against it. A low moan climbs up my throat, and I find my hips rocking against his, looking for friction to ease the growing ache between my legs. Sterling leaves a trail of kisses from my jaw, down my neck, over my shoulder. His fingers slide inside the robe and trace over my skin, his hand pressing on my belly as a shudder works through him.

I take his hand and slide it lower into the waistband of my shorts. He takes the clue and I lift up on my knees so he can slide his finger through my core. "Sterling," I breathe, head falling back. He nips at his mark again, making my hips jerk.

Sterling works his finger over my clit before sliding two fingers inside. I moan at the stretch and sensation of being filled, but I know it can be so much more than that. His fingers pale in comparison to the cock that strains the confines of his costume. I drop my hand from his shoulder to his pants and palm his hardness, making him hiss against my neck.

"Fuck, kitten," he groans. "Stand up."

My legs shake as I push to my feet, using his shoulder to leverage me. Sterling wastes no time tugging my shorts down my legs and I step out of them, letting him toss them to the side.

Before I can sit back on his lap, Sterling grabs my thighs and forces me to stand wider. The cool air on my heated center makes me gasp, and I gasp again when Sterling's tongue slides through to my clit.

"Oh gods, Sterling." I knot my fingers in his hair, pressing him closer as I rock my hips against his face.

His hands holding my thighs, and my fingers in his hair are the only things holding me up. My legs shake and tremble, each lick of his tongue against my clit builds the pleasure inside me, threatening to push me over the edge.

His icy eyes meet my gaze, the blue darker than usual with his blown pupils. "You taste different," he breathes, licking his lips with a feral grin. "It's fucking addicting."

He renews his vigorous ministrations on my core until I'm panting and grasping the top of his head to support myself. Heat flutters through me, spreading out from my core to warm my entire body. Even the hoot of a nearby owl isn't enough to pull me away from my mate and his tongue.

"Sterling," I gasp, clutching his hair tighter. "I'm so close."

He pulls away with a wicked grin, his lips shining with my arousal. "Well, I guess I should slow down then."

A whine of protest climbs up my throat, and I attempt to push his head back between my legs. He resists with a low laugh that slithers over my skin. My attempts cease when he reaches to his waistband and lifts his hips, pulling his pants down his thighs. His cock springs free, already hard and weeping for me. I drop to my knees hard enough to cause me to hiss as rocks dig into my skin, but I don't care. I want Sterling's cock inside me. Now.

Sterling grasps my face and kisses me, letting me taste myself on his tongue. As I rock my hips, rubbing my core over his cock, he bites my lower lip hard enough to draw blood. A low rumbling growl echoes through the woods and it takes me a moment to realize it's coming from him.

"Can you tell from my blood?" I ask, a touch breathlessly.

His fingers dig into my hips, and he lifts me so he's perched right at my entrance. "Yes. Your scent." He slowly slides in an inch. "Your cum." Another inch. "Your blood." Another inch. "Everything screams at me that my mate is pregnant." He pulls me down hard the last inches, and I gasp. "My wolf went fucking crazy as soon as I scented it on you." He lifts me to slide out as far as he can, only to pull me back down again. "Our mate. Our pup."

Each word is punctuated by a thrust of his hips as he lifts me and pulls me down again and again. Each word is low and filled with a growl I know comes straight from his wolf. Each word coils in my belly, fanning the flames of my desire until I'm sure I'll combust.

"Don't stop," I beg, digging my fingers into his shoulders hard enough to leave marks. "Please, don't stop."

Another growl vibrates his chest. "Never."

And then he bites down on my mark and flicks his tongue over the sensitive skin. I fall apart around him, the quiet woods swallowing my scream. Sterling curses and pulls me down one last time, clutching me to his chest as he shudders through his own release.

As awareness filters back in, I find myself wrapped in his arms, my head on his shoulder. His hands gently rub my back, and I gather the energy to pull away and look at him. Those bright blue eyes that I love so much hold emotion I can't fathom.

I suck in a breath before saying something that could ruin the happiness he's found. "You're okay if the baby isn't yours?" My words are barely audible in the wind blowing through the trees. I shiver, and Sterling rubs his hands down my arms.

"It's mine. As long as the choices are between me, Cade, and Kai." A smile plays about his lips, laughter lighting his eyes.

I smack his chest. "Of course those are the only options. Like I could handle another guy. You three are enough."

He chuckles, kissing me gently. "Then that settles it. The pup is mine. It doesn't matter who technically fathered it. I'll be here loving them, protecting them, spoiling them. Just as much as if it were a pup of my own."

Tears blur my vision. I know the guys all feel this way. We've talked about it a lot as we decided to try and have kids. But I couldn't stop the fear that wormed inside when our dreams became a reality. It's one thing to say you'll love a child that isn't yours, and another thing entirely to actually do it. I'm proof of that.

"Ellis, never question that. I swear to you, I will love every child you have, simply because I love you. I love Cade and Kai. I love the family we've created. And each child we have will only help to grow that love."

Another little sliver of apprehension slides away and Sterling kisses my forehead. As he helps me stand and we head back to Shari's, I can't keep the smile from my face.

Two down. One to go.

Ellis

I WAKE LATE IN THE EVENING THE NEXT DAY. BASED OFF of the scents and the bodies pressed against mine, only Cade and Kai are in bed with me. Sterling no doubt woke up earlier, despite going to bed late. He never seems to need as much sleep as the rest of us, and he usually goes for runs while we're sleeping.

I smile to myself as I think about last night and telling Sterling I'm pregnant. Seeing the joy in his eyes made emotions swell through me. I would find myself looking at him, at the happiness radiating off of him, and I would have to blink back tears. I guess the hormones are already kicking in.

Speaking of, my stomach gurgles alarmingly, and I swallow the sudden build up of saliva in my mouth. *Not now. Please just let me lay with my guys for a few more minutes.* At first, I think whoever listens to our prayers—gods, goddesses, fates, whatever —granted me my wish. I close my eyes as my stomach settles, and I focus on the arm wrapped around my belly protectively. Kai's by the coolness of his skin. Cade's leg is thrown over mine, his face buried in my neck. Waking up with them will never get old.

Just as I settle in, wrapping an arm around Kai's, my stomach lurches and I slap a hand over my mouth as I quickly jump from the bed, waking the guys. I barely make it to the bathroom before my stomach heaves, and I fall over the toilet, gripping the cool porcelain in my fingertips.

A warm hand rubs my back and gathers my hair away from my face. "Are you okay, Ellis?" Cade's voice is raspy with sleep, but the concern is obvious.

I nod my head, even as another wave of nausea doubles me over. Bile burns up my throat, and I cough and choke until I spit it in the toilet bowl. Sweat clings to my skin, and I rest my forehead on the cool tile floor as I catch my breath. It seems to have passed.

When I sit up, drawing my knees to my chest, Cade's eyes search mine. "Ellis?"

"I must have a bug or something," I say hoarsely.

Cade helps me to my feet and hovers while I brush my teeth. When I'm done, he wraps an arm around my waist. "Come on. Let's get you settled back in bed."

Kai has left, probably figuring I'll want privacy with Cade while I divulge my secret. I let Cade mother hen me, pulling back the covers and plumping the pillows. Once I'm settled and comfortable, he sits next to me.

"Can I double check?" He holds out his hands, violet light sparkling at his fingertips. "Just to make sure it's nothing serious?"

Biting back a smile, I nod. I watch his face closely, wanting to see every reaction that passes across his features as he realizes what the cause of my sickness is. His hands grip my face gently, the warmth of his magic spreading through me. I have to battle to keep my eyes open against the comforting sensation. But when his magic travels to my stomach, it halts.

Cade's purple eyes go impossibly big, and they dart to my belly as his mouth falls open. The warmth increases as he sends more magic to the little bundle growing inside of me. When he looks at me, his eyes shimmer with unshed tears.

"Ellis," he breathes. "Ellis, you're ..."

I smile and nod, taking his hands in mine, but leaving them

on my stomach. "Yes." Just one word. That's all it takes for him to suck his magic back into himself and drop his head to my belly.

His breath is harsh as he exhales, the warmth skittering over my naked skin. "Oh my gods," he breathes, sitting up and looking at my stomach like he can see inside. "I'm going to be a dad?"

"You are." I sit up and cup his cheeks, drawing his attention to my face. "You, Kai, and Sterling are going to be daddies." And amazing dads they will be. I already know this for a fact.

Cade's brow furrows, and for a second, doubt creeps in. Then he says, "If he or she is Kai's, I'm going to be pissed he beat me to it. He'll never let me and Sterling live it down." But there is a glimmer in his eyes that eases the anxiety.

I laugh, because he's right. If this baby is biologically Kai's, no one will hear the end of how powerful his sperm is that it was the first to impregnate me. Cade cuts the laugh off with a kiss.

"This is ... I'm ..." he shakes his head, smiling ruefully. "I don't even know what to say."

"Don't say anything. Just kiss me."

Cade does exactly that. He climbs over me, making sure to keep his weight from squashing me, and he claims my mouth. Immediately, my hormones flare to life, and I'm more than ready for him. Ever since I found out I was pregnant, I've been incredibly horny. Hornier than usual.

My nipples are extra sensitive, and when Cade rubs his thumb over one, I arch my back and moan. He chuckles darkly, and I watch his violet eyes turn navy as his pupils expand. When he trails kisses down my neck and over my chest, I thread my fingers in his hair and push him lower.

He complies without any banter, and wraps his mouth around one nipple, tongue flicking, while his fingers toy with my other nipple. Within seconds I'm writhing under him, trying to rub my body against his. But he keeps himself just out of reach. A whimper climbs up my throat, and I fist the sheets to prevent myself from smacking him.

"Please, Cade. I need to feel you inside me." My voice barely sounds like mine. It's so husky and full of want. "Please, please, please." The word tumbles from my lips, over and over like a mantra, and I squirm and thrash my head as he continues to lavish my nipples until they are so sensitive I might cry.

With agonizing slowness he releases my nipple then grins at me. "Be patient, love." He slides down between my thighs, but pauses to press a soft kiss to my belly and the baby growing inside me. He whispers something, but it's too quiet to hear, then kisses my stomach again.

When he looks up and meets my gaze, his eyes burn and it makes me shiver. Fingers dig into my thighs and spread my legs roughly. Cade's look turns feral, and a low growl rumbles in his chest. By the time he lowers his head to my core, I'm practically panting with anticipation and need.

The first swipe of his tongue draws a long, low moan from me, and the sound seems to spur Cade on. He doubles his efforts, licking and nipping, completely devouring me. My hips lift, searching for more of him, and I grind myself against his face. Cade's fingers dig into my hips, pulling me closer, and I love the bite of pain that tempers the pleasure.

"Don't stop," I beg. "Please don't stop. I'm so ..." My words trail off into a moan as fire lights inside of me and spreads through my entire body. I clamp Cade's head between my thighs and arch my back as my orgasm rolls through me in wave after wave of pleasure.

Cade doesn't stop until I lay limply on the bed, sucking in breath and trying to calm my racing heart. When he looks at me, with his lips and chin glistening, my core clenches. He's so fucking sexy with that glazed look in his eyes and his hair mussed from my fingers. I love this side of him. The side that steers away from the sweet and caring mage that he is everyday to become the seductive man I need in the bedroom.

Cade's body radiates heat as he hovers over me, lowering his mouth to mine so I can taste myself on his lips. Despite the orgasm I just had, I'm ready for more. He doesn't make me wait for it. Cade lines up with my entrance and holds my gaze as he slowly pushes inside.

His rhythm is slow and sensual at first, his strokes long and lazy. It's as if he's reminding me of his love, of the first time we had sex in the shower. I'd fallen then. And he'd caught me. He'd caught every single time since. But Cade quickly realizes I need more than that. I know he loves me, and I know he'll always catch me when I fall. Right now, I need him to destroy me.

And he does.

Cade's thrusts become wild and hard. I grasp the sheets in my hands, twisting them as he pounds into me and shoves me further up the bed until my head hits the headboard. He doesn't stop. A wicked sort of possession has overcome him, making his eyes glow with violet light. It's like he's making sure I know I belong to him, no matter whose baby I'm growing in my belly.

The fire lights in my gut, spreading outward until I'm burning all over. "Oh gods, Cade!"

"Not yet," he growls. "Don't even think about it."

I want to laugh, but it comes out as a strangled sob. I'm on the precipice looking over at the fall beneath me, and I'm hanging on by one finger. "Cade," I whine.

He grins at me, and his magic slithers over his chest and down his body until it wraps around my clit and squeezes. There is no holding back after that. I scream his name as my vision goes white and my body seizes. Each wave crashes through me, unending and euphoric. And when I finally slump to the bed, Cade kisses me gently before slamming home once more, shuddering and breathing my name onto my neck.

I'm covered in sweat. My limbs shaky and weak. But my heart is soaring in my chest. Cade rolls me over to sprawl on top of him, and I listen to his heartbeat begin to slow. This man is going to be a father. He's going to help raise the child I'm carrying. A goofy grin spreads across my face, and I'm glad he can't see it.

Kai pokes his head in the room, one pierced brow raised high. "Are you finished? Can I come back to bed now?"

Cade huffs. "Yes, you can."

Kai jumps into the bed, making me squeal, and he tackles both me and Cade. "Mmm," he hums, snuggling into us. "This is perfect."

"It's only missing one thing," Sterling says, stepping in the room with a grin. He quickly strips to his boxers and climbs into bed with us. Kai moves to lay next to Cade while Sterling plasters himself against my back. He nuzzles my neck, inhaling my scent, and his wolf rumbles in contentment. "Now it's perfect."

It is. It is absolutely perfect. With my three Shields surrounding me, our child growing inside of me, this is the life I've dreamed of for myself. And these guys have made sure it's come true.

And it's only the start. I can't wait to see where else this dream goes. As long as my family is with me, it'll be perfect.

Acknowledgments

I still hate writing these things. But I'll acknowledge my usuals.

Thank you to the readers who have enjoyed these characters as much as I have. Ellis and her men hold a special place in my heart. Saying goodbye was too hard, so I had to give you all a glimpse into their future. I hope you enjoy it.

My hubby, my protector, my sounding board, my partner. Thank you for all of the extra support you give you me for this crazy writing adventure I have found myself on.

To my Midnight Publishing Family. Once again, I'm here because of the constant support and love I get from you guys. Thank you!

To Lou, my writing wife, my bestie, my little gremlin friend. Thanks for keeping me sane through the chaos.

About the Author

Whitney L. Spradling is a neurospicy, full-time Occupational Therapist and autism mama, who has had a dream to write and publish a novel since she was a little girl. She lives outside of Cincinnati with her husband, son, and two cats.

She is a strange mixture of Disney adult, elder emo, and board game nerd with a love of tattoos, skulls, moths, bees, Gengar, and otters.

When she is not writing, she can be found in her craft room making custom tumblers, or curled up with a good book and a cup of coffee (or glass of wine).

more information on how *Hunters of Ironport* and *Witches of Moondale* fit together please visit the author's website.

***

Heat Of Seas by DeAnna Hill

SOME ARE LED BY DESIRE.

After the mysterious death of the kingdom's queen ushers in a deadly plague, Carnaxa, Princess of Antalis, is promised to a rival kingdom. As ancient prophecies unfold, not only is Carnaxa in danger, but the fate of her kingdom as well.

Meanwhile, Anara, a gift of sorts and nothing more, was taken from her homeland. She didn't realize giving her heart away would keep her emotionally shackled, mirroring the physical chains she wore.

OTHERS ARE LED BY DUTY.

Captain Thylas has guarded Carnaxa since the day he washed ashore. When he's asked to accompany her to marry another, he finds himself torn between serving his kingdom and the desires of his heart.

Ereon, the Prince of Shaston, was raised in blood and battle. Faced with an uncompromising demand, he must choose between his birthright and his destiny.

WHEN DESIRE AND DUTY CLASH, LEGENDS ARE MADE.